Door County Novellas

Volume One

Christmas in July
&
In Plain Sight

LEIGH MORGAN

Pen & Sword publishing

This is a work of fiction. Names, characters, places, brands, media, and incidents are either the product of the author's imagination or are used fictitiously. The author acknowledges the trademarked status and trademark owners of various products referenced in this work of fiction, which have been used without permission. The publication/use of these trademarks is not authorized, associated with, or sponsored by the trademark owners.

Cover design by Vincent Milewski

Also by Leigh Morgan

Second Chances

Sparring Partners
Book 1 of The Warrior Chronicles

Fighting Fate
Book 2 of The Warrior Chronicles

Defending Destiny
Book 3 of The Warrior Chronicles

A Potter's Woods Christmas

Midday Masquerade

Second Chance Wedding

Heather of His Heart

Also by Leigh Morgan (writing as M.L. MacDonald)

Home Again

Christmas
In
July

Dedication

First, to all Naturopaths – Thank you.

I am thankful to Krystal at Everything About Dance, in Milwaukee, for taking a risk on a mother and son tap duo and for making our lives more joy-filled.

Special thank you to Colin O'Brien for introducing me to the moving sensuality that is Rumba. You made Maddy and Drew work. Just goes to show, sometimes simply showing up for dance makes wonderful things happen.

CHAPTER ONE

July
154lbs.

Seven Daily Meditations, Thirty minutes—fifteen-minute morning and evening sessions—of personal journaling, one-mile walking with the General, no chocolate, introduction of kale to diet.

July in Fish Creek was where joy went to die.

Madelyn Grace was sure of it.

Madelyn grew up in *the Door*, as Door County, Wisconsin, was known to the few locals who populated it year-round. Fish Creek in the summer, July in particular, was mostly populated with tourists. Wealthy Illinoisans created a sizeable percentage of the visitors, some of whom had second, sometimes third homes here, as well as boats. Big boats. They subsidized the economy, and they knew it. They drove up home prices, and they didn't consider what that might mean for everyone else.

The Door was built on service, and the tourists demanded and got serviced. Regularly.

Wild horses and a crate filled with colored diamonds couldn't have gotten Madelyn to move back to Fish Creek. It took her daughter establishing a naturopathic medical practice here to do the impossible. Now that she was back in a place she'd swore never to return to, her daughter no longer seemed to have the time nor the inclination to be with her.

"Stop feeling sorry for yourself and go do something productive," Madelyn said out loud to herself. It was far from her usual morning meditation which was supposed to help her greet the day with joy, hope, and the awareness that yes, she did have the power to make her life the wonderful adventure she dreamed it could be.

Madelyn was supposed to be repeating: *In small moments, great achievements are built. Success comes in compiling enough small moments.* Since it was 7:30 and all she'd collected so far was the General's *small* piles of poo, Madelyn decide it was time to grab the General, stop feeling sorry for herself, and walk a mile before the tourists realized it was time to wake up.

…

"Hey, Drew, Maddy's walking that rat terrier of hers again," said Sam Wittaker, Drew's deputy. "Right on schedule. Every day since she got back two weeks ago. 7:30—time to walk. How many more weeks are you going to let her walk by without talking to her?"

Drew ignored the younger man's grin and looked at his watch: *7:32.* Maddy was two minutes later than usual, so technically, she wasn't right on schedule. All he said to Sam was, "Time for coffee. See you in a bit."

Sam chuckled.

Drew reached for the baseball cap he'd insisted the town adopt as part of his uniform and started walking. He knew Maddy's route by heart, and he still hadn't approached her. Every time he saw her, his heart thudded painfully in his chest like it used to in high school when she'd walk by. Maddy loved him then. Every bit as much as he'd loved her. Drew was sure of it.

Until she ran away.

Drew still didn't know what made her leave. He couldn't fathom why she'd stayed away for twenty-five years. And he didn't know what brought her back, but he was fairly certain it had something to do with the new medical clinic just outside of town, aptly named Grace Medical. Hard for a police chief worth his salt to miss that connection. Drew wondered what the tagline "For All Your Naturopathic Needs" meant. He'd find out before he made an appointment for his yet undiagnosed naturopathic needs, the symptoms of which he started researching online so he could go there more than once if he needed to. He had to come up with something that wasn't too severe and couldn't be cured by a simple, *drink more green tea and call me in a month*. Of course, he could just stop in and say hello, introduce himself, and offer to patrol more regularly in the event the new clinic's owner needed assistance. But that wouldn't help him understand the subtleties of how the newest member of the Grace family earned her living.

Grace Medical's signage also indicated in very small

print "Some emergency medical service provided as needed." Drew had no idea what kind of emergency merited naturopathic care, and he was in no hurry to find out. Still, it was nice to have a doctor nearby when the closest emergency center was in Sturgeon Bay, miles away with one main road in and out.

Little did Drew Selleck know how manifestly those small seven words printed on Grace Clinic's front door would forever alter his life.

What Drew Selleck did know was that today Maddy Grace was going to talk to him. Whether or not he had to arrest her to make it happen was totally up to her.

CHAPTER TWO

"Come on, General. How about I lead today, and you walk beside me for a change?" Madelyn stopped.

General kept on walking, stretching his leash taut. It was a bungie leash and he knew exactly how far he could stretch it before it tugged him back. This had become habit too—the General leading until Madelyn wore the little guy out. "Just thought we'd try it the normal way for once, buddy. Silly me."

"You were many things, Maddy, including silly when the occasion called for it. I doubt you're silly now."

Madelyn whirled around, bringing the little General with her. Her free hand moved to her chest reflexively, right over her heart. Her quick inhalation of breath drew a smile from Drew.

"Good to know I can still take your breath away, Maddy."

"Don't call me that," Madelyn said more sharply than she intended. Drew had that effect on her. She saw those bright-blue eyes and her mind filled with images of skinny-dipping in Old Man Johnson's pond. It was those memories and what came after that had gotten her trouble in the first place. Self-preservation made Madelyn drop her hand, straighten her spine, and repeat yesterday's mantra: *You are a strong independent woman. Your life is your own. You do not need a man to complete you. You are a strong independent woman.*

...

By the third time, Madelyn almost convinced herself she believed it. She was strong. She was independent. She didn't need a man, but sure as the sun rises in the east, she still wanted Drew. Apparently, time and distance hadn't muted that ache. The problem was Drew wouldn't want her when he found out the truth. Then she'd watch that kind, gentle teasing leave his eye.

Oh, why had I risked coming home?

Because Julie's here, she scolded herself, *and you crave a relationship with your adult daughter. So, suck it up, buttercup, and don't get distracted by an older set of blue eyes with engaging crinkles at the corners. Who cares if he's even more handsome than he'd been at eighteen?*

It took Drew asking, "What would you like me to call you?" to get Madelyn to follow their first conversation in over twenty-five years. She wasn't seventeen and so in love she couldn't think of anything or anyone but Drew anymore. She was a grown professional woman with a grown-up professional name. "Madelyn. It's been Madelyn for two decades now," she said.

General chose that moment to approach Drew and lay down at his feet. Drew bent to scratch behind the Westie's ears. As soon as Drew hit a full crouch, Madelyn's little traitor rolled over for a belly rub. Her best friend who was generally indifferent with strangers bonded with the one man Madelyn needed to be estranged from.

She wasn't sure why she did it. Especially seeing the joy that man and dog were sharing. But Drew wanted to pretend there was no distance between them that couldn't be bridged with a smile and polite conversation. All she could think of was the need to get away before she said something intimate.

"Madelyn Nelson was my married name," she said. Why she said it, she didn't know since she'd been using Madelyn Grace professionally for years.

Drew stopped petting General. He stood slowly, no longer smiling. Madelyn could read his expression, and she sensed his anger and his sympathy. The anger she expected. The sympathy she did not. But that was Drew, honest with his emotions and not afraid to share them.

"I knew you married. Ruby told me."

Count on Aunt Ruby to share the news. At that moment, Madelyn wanted to strangle her well-meaning aunt.

Drew took a step closer as General came back to her side, cocking his head at each one of them in turn, sensing his newfound friend's tension, as well as hers. "I was sorry to hear of your husband's death."

The sincerity in Drew's eyes made Madelyn feel small for having used her dead husband to put distance between herself and the first man who owned her heart. "Thank you," is all she could manage to say.

"Don't thank me, Maddy," Drew said harshly. "And don't expect me to call you by another man's name. Even a dead one. You are Maddy Grace to me. Then and now. Forever."

His words shook her to her core. Drew as a boy would never have spoken to her like that. In fact, the only time she could remember him being serious with her was the first time he told her he loved her.

Drew looked at her for seconds that lasted far longer than they should have.

Then he tipped his hat and turned to walk away.

Madelyn stopped him. "Drew, I—"

"Don't say anything you don't mean, Maddy." He laughed harshly, and the sound hurt her ears. "In fact, don't say anything at all." He looked at her over his shoulder and said so quietly that she almost missed it, "I won't let you disappear on me again. I'll see you every day until you finally admit you don't want to let me go again."

This time when he walked away, Madelyn let him go. Drew Selleck had rendered her speechless, embarrassed by her behavior, and eager to see him again. It was the last one that frightened her most.

Drew had managed to speak with Maddy, *call me Madelyn*, without arresting her. A monumental feat after she threw her dead husband's name at him. He'd call her by that name only after he was dead. Not even then, he silently amended. He planned to be holding Maddy close throughout eternity, *after* she took his name. Maddy Selleck.

It had a nice ring to it.

The memory of her face when he told her he'd be seeing her every day brought a smile back to his face. She'd been afraid, appalled, and just for a moment after her eyes flared, excited. That flash of the old Maddy had him whistling all the way back to the office.

CHAPTER THREE

Ruby Grace Hodgkins had just about enough of her niece and grandniece. Maddy was overbearing, and Julie was as stubborn as her mother and bound to outdo her mother in audacity. Julie was an ungrateful child, something no twenty-four-year-old doctor should be. That wasn't quite fair, Ruby silently amended. Julie Grace was plenty grateful to everyone *except* her mother.

It was well past time to change that, Ruby thought. She'd done all she could getting Julie to settle in Fish Creek, a chore made easier by leasing a building to her grandniece at a price no new doctor could turn down without being stupid. Julie wasn't stupid, just stubborn as the day was long—and immature.

Ruby had already buried two husbands by the time she was Julie's age. Ruby loved them both, but she'd have served the second one arsenic had he not fallen off the tractor tilling their small field and done the deed himself. No one deserved to be beaten simply for the sin of being born female.

After the death of her second husband, Ruby had had quite enough of the male species and decided to move up to the Door to be closer to her sister, Opal. Opal married a decent man, a homebody who loved her and their child. He made cherry wine and fished when it suited him, until Lake Michigan took him and Opal both after turning particularly surly on what had been a lovely afternoon in September 1984. They left Ruby with an orchard to run and a nine-year-old child to raise. Ruby still thanked her Maker each and every day that Maddy wasn't with them that fate-filled day. Her sweet Maddy.

God had taken two gentle souls but left the sweetest among them for a jaded spinster to raise. Ruby had been more than blessed. Maddy, the dear soul, had not been.

Ruby was bound and determined to see her Madelyn happy. Ruby had her place in heaven to secure after all, and there was no way God was opening those gates for her without her seeing Maddy settled first. If she could mend the rift between Maddy and Julie along the way, so much the better. Maybe then God would let Ruby smack that worthless son-of-a-jackal she'd married right in his face. He deserved that. And she deserved the chance to make it happen.

Ruby's God was an Old Testament smiter when it suited Ruby for him to be.

He also sent his better angels to Earth to help old ladies like Ruby make up for what they didn't have when they were young—patience and wisdom. Ruby needed that angel now, but with or without divine intervention, Ruby was going to see Maddy settled and happy before she left this world for the next. Doc Steven's had told her she didn't have long to make it happen. Possibly by Christmas she'd be lookin' down on Maddy. Maybe a wee-bit longer than that, but not much more, Doc said.

A lot could happen between July and Christmas.

Ruby just needed it to happen a lot faster than either Maddy or Drew Selleck were moving to get the thing done. Heck, Drew spent Maddy's first two weeks in Fish Creek ogling her from afar. As for Maddy, she hadn't even given Drew so much as a second look. It wasn't lack of fire on Maddy's part. It was sheer stubbornness and fear. Probably more fear than stubbornness, but Maddy wore her fear on the inside and her stubbornness like Kevlar armor on the outside—impossible to miss and darned hard to penetrate.

Time to give Father Time an old-fashioned Grace-under-pressure nudge. Perhaps a shove would be a better use of time, Ruby amended.

Heaven was waiting, and Ruby Grace was almost ready to be called home. She had a little matchmaking to do first. Ruby sent a prayer upstairs: "You aren't going to like the shenanigans I'm about to get up to, but I haven't the time to dither around. Besides, it'll be worth it in the end. I think if you and I work together on this, we can fix what went wrong all those years ago.

"Also, if you look the other way for the next six months or so, I think you'll still want me upstairs. Especially if I ... *We* can pull this little Christmas miracle off." Ruby frowned. She probably needed to be more specific if the Almighty was going to help. "It'd probably be good if you didn't throw anymore curveballs into this situation. I'm good, but there's a limit to how far I bend my girl. I raised her, after all, and as you know, I'm not without my own issues when it comes to digging in my heels."

Ruby ended with a silent "Thanks," certain as she could be that any divine intervention would help rather than hinder her efforts.

Ruby had no way of knowing just how good the Universe in general, and the Almighty in particular, was at baseball.

CHAPTER FOUR

August
149lbs.

Five daily meditations: one upon waking, one mid-morning, one at noon, one mid-afternoon, one before bed. One piece of chocolate. Two short journaling sessions of five minutes—one after morning meditation, one after evening meditation. Two-and-a-half miles walking with the General, twice a day. Today's Mantra: Peace comes from within. Do not seek it without. -Buddha

"You did what!?" Madelyn glared at her aunt who busied herself rearranging a vase filled with marigolds Madelyn had clipped from the garden. There was another vase filled with white, red, and pink roses she'd also clipped that morning. They didn't need rearranging any more than the marigolds did, but Ruby got to work anyway. Heaven help me, Madelyn thought as she repeated her mantra of the day. Unfortunately for her, there was no peace in or out to be had.

When she was done with flowers, Ruby sat at Madelyn's

kitchen table. Was it just her imagination, or did Ruby look tired today? Madelyn wondered, her ire fleeing as she went to the refrigerator to get the pitcher of iced tea. She'd made it before her walk with the General, who was following her around this morning as if sensing her need for an ally.

Madelyn brought the PBT-free plastic pitcher and two glasses to the table. She poured a glass for Ruby and for herself, silently repeating her "inner peace" mantra while taking deep, calming breathes.

Ruby took a sip of her tea, waved a hand at Madelyn and said, "You can stop trying to breathe away what I did. It's not going to work. Drew is coming to dinner and no amount of yoga or Pilates or dog-walking is going to change that."

As irritated as Madelyn was with Ruby's constant attempts at matchmaking, she grinned at her aunt. "Exactly what do you know about Pilates?"

Ruby looked affronted. "I do yoga three mornings a week at the civic center. They have Pilates too, but I can't stand looking at all those old people trying to move around in spandex like sixteen-year-old jocks. Yoga is more my speed."

Madelyn looked at her aunt wondering when she'd missed the fact that Ruby had a life independent of her own.

Ruby got the twinkle in her eye she always got when Madelyn had failed to pull the wool over her eyes as a teenager. "I've also read a few of those 'self-help' books you've got lying around everywhere. Don't see how silently repeating 'I am the center of my Universe ... I am enough' is going to snare you a husband."

Madelyn set down her pale-blue tea mug that read "Om" on the side. She had that look she used to get whenever she thought Ruby couldn't possibly know enough to help her with her homework. "I'm forty years old—"

"—Forty-four."

"Forty-*three*, my birthday isn't for another few months. That's my point. I'm a middle-aged woman with an adult daughter and a career that's finally starting to pay more than the mortgage. I don't *need* a husband, Aunt Ruby."

"No one really *needs* a husband these days, sweetheart. Not for any of the reasons you listed anyway. Still, it's nice to wake up every morning next to your best friend."

Madelyn felt that blow to her heart far more keenly than she should have. She hoped she hid it well. "Thank goodness you're my best friend, Aunt Ruby. Better yet, you live next door, so I get to wake up and see you anytime I want."

Not for long, my darling.

Ruby finished her tea, swearing that tomorrow morning she was having espresso. What was it going to do to her that the cancer wasn't doing already? She thought about that and smiled. The espresso would make her happy, something the intruder in her body wasn't doing no matter how many of Maddy's books about "blessings" Ruby read. Seemed to Ruby, she and Maddy should stop trying to find the blessings in life and just start living it. Every blessed moment of it.

Ruby looked at her watch she didn't need, not with the new phone Maddy bought for her when she got her artist in residence job. Ruby had just gotten used to the old one, but apparently these things needed to be replaced every two years. One thing Ruby was certain they didn't have in heaven were cell phones that constantly displayed the time to the second, and email that was dutifully time stamped, just in case one was tracking the seconds. Why would anyone need to know the exact seconds in the day or the number of minutes for that matter?

"I've signed us up for tap dancing lessons—ninety minutes a day until Thanksgiving," she told Madelyn. "Then we're doing a number in the Thanksgiving Gala. You can shop for dinner after we dance."

Something in the nonchalant way Ruby was acting seemed almost desperate to Maddy. Ruby did unexpected and sometimes crazy things in the moment, but Ruby always had a reason, even if Madelyn couldn't immediately see it. "I don't have tap shoes," Madelyn said.

Ruby's grin lit up her face. A small woman to begin with, she had shrunk with age. But when she smiled, she seemed six feet tall and ready to take on the world. "You're shoes and your fedora are in the car."

Madelyn returned Ruby's smile. "Ah, what the hell. I always wanted to take tap dancing lessons."

Ruby didn't do stern well. "Language, young lady. ... And I remember. Couldn't get dance lessons for you then, but I can now. So now is when we're going to do it."

. . .

Old adages and sailor's wisdom were alive and well in

the Door. Some of them had proven true over the decades of J.T. Selleck's life. Some were hogwash, and dangerous hogwash at that. That bit about "Red sky at night, sailor's delight. Red sky in the morning, sailors take warning" was true in his experience. The twaddle about women being bad luck on commercial fishing boats did not have any basis whatsoever in reality. In J.T.'s opinion, that bit of dubious wisdom could have substituted "red-headed men over six feet tall" for "women" and been just about as accurate.

The colloquial—and far outdated—adage that men and women couldn't be friends, also stuck in J.T.'s craw.

He'd been friends with his wife since the day he first pulled her pigtails in second grade until the day she died of ovarian cancer just before her thirty-ninth birthday. The mutual enjoyment of their physical relationship didn't hurt the love they shared. It didn't define it either. J.T. loved Mary long before their wedding night, and he loved her long after they could no longer be intimate. He loved Mary still.

But Mary was no longer his best friend. Ruby Grace Hodgkins held that honor, and damned if his Maker wasn't going to take Ruby away from him too.

"Everyone dies, J.T. Everyone. Stop feeling sorry for yourself and start making Ruby's wishes come true," J.T. said out loud. He'd recently begun talking to himself whenever strong emotion crept up and hit him over the head. He talked to himself frequently when he took the boat out. His grandfather had taught him that. No place on earth was better to have frank discussions with the

Almighty than the open sea or the Great Lakes. That kind of venue seemed to open a direct line to the heavens. Open water was the perfect microcosm of life—beautiful; expansive; peaceful; and viciously violent, depending on the whims of Mother Nature; giving in its bounty, and taking life when it suited. Beautiful. Arbitrary. Capricious. That was life on the water. As J.T. got older, he'd come to see that as the mainstay of life—period.

That wasn't how Maddy Grace saw life.

Madelyn Grace saw ghosts and added them to her work, beautiful wisps of color populating places they loved, like they had in earlier times. Maddy's work made J.T. feel whole and thankful for every moment he'd been lucky enough to spend in the Door.

He was also quite good at picking investments. Maddy's work was going to make him a mint. That he loved her and her aunt didn't make its way into his decision to grant Maddy the artist in residency position at the coveted Door County Artist's Retreat. But it didn't hurt his bottom line either.

J.T. started collecting Maddy's paintings and prints the second they became available for sale. He didn't have everything she'd done, but his collection was substantial. So substantial, that he'd opened The John Thomas Gallery in Fish Creek, specializing in local artists and maritime artists from around the world. Prints were his biggest sellers, primarily because they were the most affordable, but he sold originals as well. Drew's deputy, Sam, created an online gallery for J.T., and the sales from that alone produced enough for J.T. to comfortably retire anytime the notion suited him. It didn't suit him yet, and probably never would, so long as he had the hope of grandchildren.

Thoughts of grandchildren inevitably led to Julie Grace. How his son couldn't see his eyes shining out of that girl's lovely face, J.T. couldn't fathom. Drew saw connections where very few did, yet that boy refused to see what was right in front of his face. No doubt blinded by Maddy Grace. Drew never could see past Maddy when she was around.

Well past time to find that son of his and set the man to action. The way Drew was moving, he'd grow old alone, pining for a woman he'd loved since second grade. Why did daring seem to end at forty?

J.T. walked past his gallery, manned by one of the artists he sponsored—a brilliant young man who had the misfortune to favor wearing his hair in a bun, held back with chopsticks. J.T. headed toward The Rooster for breakfast.

"Morn'n, J.T." Anne Gallager was a handsome woman of about sixty who J.T. had been thinking about asking out for the past year. "Drew's in the back, if you're look'n for him. I'll bring coffee and a roll right over." Then she winked at him.

Anne's cinnamon rolls were going to be the death of him. J.T. didn't have the heart to tell her he didn't particularly like them. "How about just coffee, eggs, and toast today, Anne."

J.T. found Drew grinning over his coffee mug, remnants of his breakfast potatoes cluttering the table. "Why don't you just tell Anne you don't like cinnamon?

Better yet, ask the woman out already. You've been making eyes at her for over a year."

J.T. slid into the booth across from his son. "I haven't been 'making eyes' at anyone," J.T. flushed knowing he had.

Drew nodded toward the counter where Bill Haviland sat. A wealthy retiree from one of Chicago's northern suburbs, the man was tall, thinner than J.T., and at least a decade younger. It didn't hurt that Bill was genuinely likable either. "Bill's been stepping up his game. He's asked Anne to the concert tonight on the Green. She hasn't answered yet."

Anne chose that moment to deliver a steaming mug of coffee and an enormous cinnamon roll that sold well with the tourists. The gleam in her eye should have warned him. "John Thomas Selleck, when are you going to admit you can't stand my muffins. Everyone in the place knows you secretly throw them in bathroom wastebasket when you think I'm not look'n."

Drew watched his father squirm, turn an interesting shade of pink, then rise to the challenge. "It's not your muffins I can't stand, Anne. It's these cloying gobs of cinnamon dough drenched in diabetes-inducing sugar icing."

His father put the roll back on Anne's tray and gave the woman a smile Drew was sure Bill Haviland could feel from across the room. "Your muffins suit me just fine, Anne. How about going to the concert tonight with me? I'll take you to Serendipity beforehand. I hear their new chef does a killer plank salmon."

Anne flushed at J.T.'s less than subtle appreciation for

her curves. She wasn't embarrassed; she was pleased. Drew could tell by the way she held her tray in one hand and gently back-handed J.T. with the other.

"Well, you're about five minutes too late, J.T. I just told Bill I'd join him for dinner and the concert tonight."

Bill lifted his coffee mug in a mock salute that had Drew feeling like shaking the man. He couldn't imagine exactly how is father felt now that J.T. had finally taken the plunge and asked Anne out on a date. J.T. had a lady in Sturgeon Bay he saw off and on that no one was supposed to know about, but that wasn't something that would lead to happily-ever-after. It was more of a mutual convenience that saw far more starlight than daylight.

"How about the weekend then? Maybe a picnic and a sail? Weather is supposed to be beautiful on Saturday."

Anne beamed at J.T., and Drew could feel his father relax.

Drew looked at Bill, who'd set his coffee down and wasn't trying to hide his displeasure.

"It's a date, John Thomas. I just happen to have the entirety of the weekend off," Anne said as she turned and walked away. The second she turned toward the counter, the smile returned to Bill's eyes. He called Anne over, and she laughed heartily at something Bill said.

"Bill's going to give you a run for your money, Dad."

"Wouldn't be half as smart as the gossips give him credit for if he didn't pursue Anne. Don't know why it's taken me so long to ask."

Drew said nothing when his father gave him the long stare. It was clear they weren't talking about Anne Gallager any longer.

Madelyn and Ruby Grace took that moment to walk into the Rooster. J.T. caught a glimpse of Julie Grace jogging up the sidewalk on her way in to join her mother and her aunt. Before they could be seated elsewhere, J.T. got up and pulled a chair to the end of the booth. The Rooster's booths were designed to hold six people. Five would be no problem.

"Dad—"

J.T. heard Drew call after him. A warning to stop right now, in what should have been a term of endearment.

J.T. ignored him.

CHAPTER FIVE

"Good morning, ladies. I've saved a seat for you," J.T. said, beaming first at Ruby, then at Maddy. He reserved his most heart-breaking smile for Julie, the young woman he wanted desperately to be his granddaughter.

The Grace women couldn't have timed it better had they planned it, and J.T. was certain they hadn't. If Ruby planned this encounter, she'd have been on the phone, ordering him to keep Drew in his seat. It was his good luck that Ruby took his lead and made a beeline for the booth before Drew could shuffle his way out.

"I'll take it as a personal affront, Drew, if you try to leave before I've had my breakfast," Ruby said, shooing him back into the booth before he could make a gracious exit. "You wouldn't want to be rude to an old woman, now would you, Sheriff?"

"I'm the police chief, Ruby, not the sheriff."

"Oh, well, you both carry badges, don't you? You're also here to serve the public. I'm the public right now, Drew Selleck."

Drew didn't bother substituting *shield* for *badge*. He'd learned long ago that kind of unsolicited correction only made the women in his life angry. Even his secretary insisted on using the word badge just to irritate him after he'd made the mistake of correcting her.

Ruby had him on the issue of public service though, and she was sly enough to bring out that part of his law enforcement duties. That was one of the reasons he ate breakfast in the community he served at least a few times a week. Drew was simply grateful Ruby let the "service" meme die. He didn't need to be thinking about "servicing" when Maddy's perfume was weaving its way around him, and he was close enough to see the golden circle around her hazel irises. Drew's memories didn't do the beauty of Maddy's eyes any justice. Drew forced himself to look away before he said something poetic and completely out of place.

He looked at Ruby thinking she'd be a safe harbor in what was gearing up to be stormy water. No such luck.

The look Ruby shot him told him she knew exactly what he was thinking, and she'd light a candle and play Barry White over the P.A. system if she thought she could move him closer to Maddy. Drew almost choked on his ice water as he registered Ruby's wink. She was a Sunday school teacher for goodness' sake, not a madam at some G-rated bordello.

Perhaps these three Grace women were each more than they appeared. Drew made a mental note not to forget that bit of insight. He was sure it would serve him well in the future. If nothing else, he wouldn't be underestimating any of them. Caution would be the better part of valor. Caution had lost him Maddy once. He wasn't about to employ too much of it this time around.

Then Maddy sat down next to him and every good intention Drew had fled.

"I didn't think I'd see you until dinner," she said.

Drew nodded as Julie slid into the booth next to Ruby, who pulled her in for a quick hug before settling back. Ruby didn't even pretend interest in the menu. She simply stared between Maddy and him like an avid teenager. Julie ignored her mother and stared directly at him.

Before he could answer Maddy, Julie stuck her hand out from across the table and said, "I'm Julie Grace. Dr. Julie Grace, actually, if you're looking to refer anyone who may need an N.D., or if you ever need any naturopathic services." She cocked her head at Drew, and it reminded him of how General had cocked his head at Maddy when he wasn't sure he wanted to do what Maddy was telling him to do. *Not a good sign.*

The heart-shaped birthmark on Julie's right inner arm was clearly visible as Julie reached over the table toward Drew. Drew saw it. He shot a glance at J.T. The satisfied look in J.T.'s eyes said the mark confirmed what his father already knew. Julie was a Selleck. Drew had the same birthmark on his left wrist. His watch covered it. J.T. carried the mark on his right bicep.

The emotions flowing through Drew were myriad. They came hot, fast and burned through him like the first time he'd sunk into Maddy and made her his. The emotions began and ended with Maddy. But those in the middle were reserved for the beautiful young woman talking to him across the table.

Caution. Move with caution. There's an endgame here. Alienating Maddy or Julie will get you nowhere.

"So, you used to date my mom and now she's cooking for you. How's that going to work?"

Hopefully better than this breakfast, he thought.

Maddy looked at her daughter as if she'd grown a second head.

Drew reached out and squeezed her leg without thinking. The second he felt Maddy's warmth, she stiffened and he pulled away. He'd meant to reassure, not to irritate her further. That was part of the problem. He always wanted to make Maddy feel better. He couldn't be near her without reaching out and touching her. Right now, the two desires were at odds with one another. Drew gave a fervent prayer that that wouldn't go on forever.

Drew looked at Maddy who was now studying the Rooster's menu in minute detail. She was radiating her discomfort, but Drew sensed more than simple irritation with Julie's outlandish forwardness. Then he narrowed his eyes and answered Julie directly. *In for a penny, in for a pound.*

"Your mom and I grew up together. She was my best friend before she left Fish Creek," Drew paused. Maddy was still reading her menu. She tensed a bit when he brought up her leaving the Door. He didn't think he sounded judgmental about it, but maybe he had. He sure as the day is long was judgmental about what he was going to say next. "We dated. Exclusively. All through high school. I want to date her again. Often." Drew paused, looking into

Julie Grace's eyes. They were nothing like her mother's soft hazel. Julie's were bright, clear blue, and beautiful in their own right, but not quite as lovely as Maddy's.

He stared at Julie until she grinned and looked away. Drew needed the daughter to know he wouldn't be intimidated or put off his path by anyone. He wouldn't let anyone make Maddy uncomfortable either, not even her daughter, while he was around. If anyone was going to knock Maddy off her game, well that was going to be him. And *when* that happened, they wouldn't have an audience.

"But," Drew said turning to Maddy, who met his gaze, "tonight isn't a date. Tonight is just dinner."

Gratitude and challenge flared in Maddy's eyes.

Drew held her gaze as long as he dared, given their captive and inquiring audience, before he stood up, forcing Maddy to exit the booth. "If you'll excuse me, ladies," Drew nodded to his father, whom he briefly considered strangling. "Thanks for breakfast, Dad. I'll have Anne add it to your tab."

Drew managed to squeeze past Maddy without touching her again.

"Nice to meet you, Julie. I'll be stopping by your office soon." Drew smiled at Ruby and said to Maddy, "I'll be seeing you tonight. I'll bring dessert."

Drew put on his hat and made it out the door, managing not to look back. He met General tethered to the weeping cherry tree at the Rooster's entrance. General stood up when he saw Drew. Drew squatted to give the little guy a thorough rub behind the ears. "I'll bring dessert. What a stupid thing to say. I just can't seem to say or do anything the easy way when it comes to your mistress. How about bailing a guy out? If I do something stupid tonight, I'd really appreciate it if you'd jump up and start barking. Or you could do that goofy thing you do with your ears. Distraction. It's all about distracting the ladies from our stupidity."

Not even the General could get Drew out of the mess he was about to put himself into.

. . .

She'd been home less than a month and Madelyn was already beginning to think of herself as Maddy Grace again. That was just it. Maddy thought of Fish Creek as home. Madelyn didn't have a spot that approximated the true definition of the word. Madelyn was a wanderer. Wherever the next opportunity for a better job, a commission that would last more than a few months, or a chance to improve her education—or Julie's, that's where they moved.

After she left Fish Creek, she'd gone to live with Ruth's best friend from high school in a suburb of Minneapolis. Jackie Schneider had taken Maddy in on the condition—set by Jackie and Ruby—that Maddy get her undergraduate degree. Without Jackie Schneider's help and her aunt Ruby's financial assistance, Maddy never would have made it through college.

Yes, that meant Julie spent time in on-campus daycare. It also meant Julie had two strong women raising her and a third—Ruby—who visited often.

Julie was almost four when Maddy graduated from the University of Minnesota with a bachelor's degree in art with a minor in business. She didn't much like business, but Maddy excelled in class because she knew she had to. She also knew she didn't want to do odd jobs and wait tables for the rest of her life. It wasn't waiting tables in general that she didn't like. It was the fact that she made the most money cocktailing in higher end clubs, places where she had to fend off advances from men and women without offending them. She made good money. She learned how to negotiate her way through power plays, layered with class distinctions and clearly defined class lines. An object of desire, she was ultimately meaningless in their eyes.

Maddy made the money. Maddy paid for the best schools she could afford for Julie, and shadowed any opportunities for herself. She did everything she could to ensure Julie would have a life where she could frequent high-end cocktail clubs if she chose to, but not to work them. She didn't want Julie to suffer the indignities she had, of being groped and then having to smile as she extricated herself, politely enough to retain her employment. Maddy wanted far more for her daughter than the early life she'd chosen for herself.

And she got it. Julie was a doctor, an N.D. who graduated from medical school with honors. Maddy was intensely proud of her. And disappointed too. She'd raised a smart, independent, funny child who was also, entitled, arrogant, and casually cruel in her distain for her mother and her mother's career choices.

Maddy did what she needed to make sure Julie had

choices.

All Julie seemed to see was a mother who worked so much she was rarely around, who didn't know what it was like to earn a degree in a *real* occupation that required hard work and study. Everyone knew art wasn't any of that. Art wasn't science. Art wasn't a vocation. Art ... well, art was a hobby.

A hobby that put you through four years of undergrad, you ungrateful, entitled millennial who's never had a scheduled job besides caddying in her life.

All of this ran through Madelyn's mind as she stepped into Fish Creek's singles hot-spot: All About Dance & Yoga. The smaller print on the sign read "Salsa, Bachata, Adult ballet & Adult tap. Hot Yoga available by appointment."

The first thing Maddy saw was a long-limbed redhead with fire engine-red lips and nails. She looked like she weighed a hundred pounds, yet still managed to have sizable, propped-up breasts—and she was wrapped around Drew Selleck. The pose was decidedly sensual. One arm embraced Drew's neck as she draped across his torso.

The sleigh bells on the front door rang louder than they needed to as Ruby stepped into the dance studio behind Madelyn. The smile was still on Drew's face as he looked up to see who was coming through the door.

The woman seemed in no hurry to extricate herself from Drew's embrace as Latin music faded into silence.

The moment Drew's eyes met Maddy's, the smile drained from his face. He turned rigid and a look of embarrassed guilt washed over him. Then that, too, faded into jaw-popping stoicism.

He stared at Maddy. Silent. The sensual heat surrounding him and the woman switched quickly into awkwardness.

At least he didn't drop the woman. She let the back of her hand caress his cheek as she reluctantly moved away from Drew's embrace.

Maddy's heart beat heavily in her chest. She'd seen Drew's exhilaration and wanted to be a part of it. She'd seen the way he leaned into the woman as the final notes of music played, filling the dance studio with their haunting power of seduction.

The woman seemed to recognize Maddy, although why she would, Maddy couldn't fathom. The woman shot her gaze from Maddy to Drew, then back again. A slow deliberate smile spread across the woman's stunningly beautiful features before she turned and kissed Drew softly on the lips.

Drew did nothing to stop her, all the while holding Maddy's gaze.

It would take Maddy the better part of a week before her conscious mind realized Drew didn't kiss her back.

Maddy turned and walked out the door before the bells on the door stopped ringing. She heard Ruby say dryly, "I think Maddy's come down with the I-don't-want-to-see bug. Hopefully it's only a forty-eight-hour thing. We'll have to reschedule our lesson, Maxie. You're on your own when it comes to rescheduling dinner, Drew Selleck."

The door shutting behind Ruby didn't stop Maddy from hearing Drew's withering stream of expletives, some of which burned Maddy's ears. All of which brought some gratification.

CHAPTER SIX

Ruby rushed to catch up to Maddy. "I know you don't want to hear it, but what you're feeling right now is a good thing."

Maddy stopped in her tracks, and Ruby ran into her back. She stiffened when Ruby stumbled into her, but she didn't turn around and try to steady Ruby.

Probably a good thing, Ruby thought, steading herself. She moved around Maddy so they were standing side-by-side on the sidewalk.

"You're right. I don't want to hear it." Maddy started walking again, straight toward her tiny, white Lincoln that she'd gotten used for a song. Ruby followed, but wisely said nothing after Maddy held up one hand in the universal signal for "Stop talking before I decide to shoot you or something close enough to you that you need to fear shrapnel."

Maddy was at the driver's door, eyes closed, trying to calm her rapidly beating heart, when she heard Ruby's softly spoken words wash over her with the force of a tsunami, "You're not a teenager any longer, Madelyn Margret Grace. And you were never a coward. Until now. What exactly are you so afraid of? Being happy? Of having to actually show up and make good things happen with a man you've loved since you were in pigtails?"

Maddy let her head drift slowly to the hood of her car. She rested it there for a moment while she practiced her deep breathing exercises. This morning's snippet of enlightenment was found while randomly flipping through *Anam Cara* by John O'Donohue, a book Ruby had given her the day she moved back to Fish Creek. Today's thought was from page 83. She remembered the page because it was the year she moved to Fish Creek as a child—1983. What she recalled of this morning's passage went something like this:

To be born is to be chosen. No one is here by accident. Each one of us was sent here for a

special destiny ... In other words, a special destiny was prepared for you.

Maddy had read that and wondered if that was it then. Did it all come down to some divine providence? There was a certain freedom from guilt in that. There was a built-in excuse to continue as one started and not worry over much about creating something better with *someone* better than one thought one deserved. That's what went through Maddy's mind a 5:05 a.m. when she'd read that. Then she read this:

... But you were also given freedom and creativity to go beyond the given, to make a new set

of relationships and to forge an ever-new identity, inclusive of the old but not limited to it.

Maddy lifted her head. She looked at Ruby with a clear heart. Ruby was right. She wasn't the teenager she had been. She'd grown. She'd changed. And no matter how hard won that growth had been, it didn't change the fact that she loved Drew Selleck then and she loved the idea of him still. It was well past time to decide if she was in love with the boy he'd been or if she was interested in loving the man he'd become.

Maddy swallowed her fear, lifted her chin, and walked over to Ruby.

She bent and kissed the top of her aunt's head. "I love you, Ruby," she said quietly, filling the words with the truth of her soul. Then she placed the key-fob into Ruby's palm. "I'll be right back," she said heading purposefully back into the dance studio.

Drew and Maxie were in the corner on a black velvet settee, bent and whispering. Drew was holding Maxie's hands, but it looked more like he was restraining her than an act of intimacy. Maddy wasn't sure how she knew that, but the air surrounding them wasn't romantic in the least.

Maxie looked up the second the bells chimed.

Drew did as well, his gaze assessing and reserved, as if he was preparing for an attack. Well, Maddy thought with some satisfaction, she just might give him one.

Maddy broke eye contact with Drew although she could feel his continued appraisal. "Maxie, Ruby and I will be in tomorrow morning for our lesson and every other morning Ruby schedules. Sorry for the inconvenience of postponing today's class, but you appear to be busy filling our hour, so no harm done." *None to you, anyway.*

Then she turned to Drew whose face she could no longer read. It was as if he'd moved inside himself. He was still holding Maxie's wrists, though. When she tried to lift her hands, Drew held the woman firm, never once looking away from Maddy.

"I'll see you at six. We won't be eating in. You'll be escorting me to Alexander's. I'm warning you now, Drew Selleck. Bring your American Express card. I'm ordering oysters flown in from Maine, lobster, and a fillet the size of my palm." Maddy thought about it and added, "And probably a bottle of their best pinot noir. Myself. A bottle of my own," Maddy clarified, just to ensure he understood.

The smile he shot her was beatific.

And sultry.

The sultry hit her hard.

Maddy left without another word, head held high, before her knees gave out. Apparently audacious conduct ran deep in the Grace women. *Who knew?*

...

Drew held Maxie's hands firmly. He loved the dance, he just didn't love the dancer. He'd spent most of his life living down his "any-woman-who-cared reputation." Maxie had lived on it for as long as she'd been open.

When Maddy left, this time without turning around or coming back, Maxie stopped trying to extricate herself from Drew's grip. As soon as she did, Drew let her go, knowing she wouldn't try to reach for him again.

"Wow," she said looking at Maddy walk away. Then she

looked directly at him, and Drew saw a woman inside the shell he hadn't been introduced to yet. A no-nonsense kind of woman, he thought he'd like to get to know. "Drew Selleck, you'd be an idiot of the highest order to let that woman get away from you twice."

Then she stood up, dusted herself off, as if she'd gotten dirty sitting next to him and walked to the front door. She held it open and jerked her head toward the sidewalk. "Get going. Make it right."

Drew grinned, put his hat on, and walked to the door. "Maxie you're a better woman than you give yourself credit for," he said, meaning it.

Maxie made a rude noise then smiled conspiratorially. "That's not true. I give myself plenty of credit, most of it deserved. It's not my fault the people in this county can't see any deeper than red lipstick and painted nails."

"I see you, Maxie. And Thanks."

She shooed him out of the dance studio.

As Maxie would tell it, years later, she was the one who shooed him into a new life.

CHAPTER SEVEN

Julie Grace saw her mother exit Maxie's dance studio, lose it next to her mini SUV for some inexplicable reason, then go back into Maxie's with her chin up in the air and her shoulders stiff and erect. When Madelyn Grace got that stiff, someone was going to get shot down big-time. Julie had been on the opposite end of that more times than she cared to remember.

"My mother the drama queen. Who are you torturing now, Mother? Probably feeling the need to tell Maxie what she's doing wrong in running her business. You certainly have no filter when it comes to telling me how to run my life."

A throat cleared behind her.

Julie whirled around in time to see her part-time receptionist-cum-office-fixer-extraordinaire, Peter Blake. He leaned over the counter that doubled as his desk and smiled at her. Peter always smiled—when he wasn't looking at her in disappointment. Julie had no idea why she cared if Peter Blake, whom she *paid* to be there for goodness' sake, thought her wanting. Yet every time she was the recipient of that look, she turned hot and had to leave the room. Peter Blake was a damned nuisance, but he was also great at putting her patients, the few Julie had, at ease. Peter also did her billing, kept her charts organized, and was more than a little intuitive when it came to jotting down symptomology the patients themselves didn't disclose. Peter was smart and far too good-looking to rely on his quick wit and charm. He was also younger than she was and more self-assured (without being cocky) than anyone she'd met. There was no pretense about Peter. Peter was definitely a what-you-see-is-what-you-get kind of guy.

"Do you realize that most of the time you talk out loud, you're complaining about somebody or something?" he said.

"Do you realize that you eavesdrop far more than any polite person would admit to?"

Peter's smile grew as his eyes crinkled at the corners. "Now, you're deflecting, Doc. You're usually better than that. What's got you so off your game?" Peter came around the desk to better see what Julie saw out the front window. "Also, I don't eavesdrop. I observe and react. There's a difference."

Whatever Julie would have said to that bit of tripe flew out her ears when she heard Peter's low appreciative whistle. "Wow," he said. "Your mom looks pretty great in yoga pants."

Julie hit him.

Peter shot her a quick, if less than innocent, what-did-I-say glance, then looked back at her mom.

Julie watched Madelyn walked out of Maxie's dance studio, head held high, with a small smile on her face. Her mom even tucked a stray curl behind her ear before tossing her hair like a college cheerleader, one who knew how beautiful she was and flaunted it. Julie had to hand it to her mom. She did look good in yoga pants. Not skinny. Just good. She also looked years younger when she was smiling and unguarded like she was now. It seemed that for the last few years her mother was always guarded around her.

Maybe, just maybe, if she could connect with the not-so-perfect yet smiling Madelyn Grace, they could find common ground. Who was she kidding? Her mother would never lighten-up enough with her to connect in any meaningful way. Julie wasn't sure why she felt that as a loss, but she did. Suddenly she was jealous of whoever it was that made her mom's face light up.

"Yeah, well, looks can be deceiving," Julie said. "Mom just isn't a happy person."

Peter looked at her quite seriously. "If that smile is deceiving, and I were twenty years older, I'd be more than willing to be deceived."

"You're disgusting," Julie said, not believing it. Her mom looked good. She looked happy. Why hadn't Julie seen the face her mother now showed the world? Just like Peter, her mom was more than she presented to Julie.

Peter lost his smile. "No, Doc. I'm honest. You'd be happier and a lot less judgmental if you ever bothered to give honesty a whirl. Maybe it's time you stopped blaming your mom for everything you see as negative in your life. Give her a break."

Julie didn't miss the fact that she'd criticized her mother for doing just that minutes ago—and left the room. She *did* blame her mom for most of her negative experiences, and some of that blame, her mom had earned. But Julie's ears got hot when she admitted to herself she may have gone too far. She'd been blaming her mom for so long for everything she could, she hadn't stopped to think how far she'd pushed away the one person who loved her unconditionally.

Julie didn't like introspection. She pushed the nagging thought away. Then she blamed Peter for making it pop into her brain in the first place. Life was simpler without Peter pointing out her faults.

"Damn you, Peter. And the horse you rode in on."

Peter's amused voice washed over her from the other room. "I heard that."

Of course, he did. Julie pushed herself deeper into the case file she was reading. Mrs. Weatherby was having trouble sleeping. *That* Julie could do something about.

CHAPTER EIGHT

Madelyn felt lighter than she had in years. Simply engaging with Drew and not fearing her every word, brought a kind of relief mingled with anticipation for the first time since the summer after high school.

Maddy's heart sped up at the thought of a dinner date that didn't involve a blind date set up by her perpetually romance-obsessed agent. No one else in her small sphere of acquaintances cared whether Madelyn dated or not. Except Ruby. Ruby wanted her married and what Ruby called *settled,* yesterday.

Madelyn was as settled as she was likely to get. Settled was overrated and under scorned. Settled would kill her if she didn't shake things up in her life. Settled was the same as giving up and admitting that the best of what you were, and what you might have been had your dreams come true, was behind you. Settled meant stocking up on canned food, getting a cat from the local shelter, and relying on Twitter and Facebook feeds to vicariously experience someone else's adventure.

Screw that.

Maddy opened her computer as she sipped her Feel Invigorated herbal tea. It was time for her daily mantra. She'd signed up for a daily positive thought that came right to her home screen. It was a way to focus her mind and bring about some positive action on her part. She had numerous books and a few magazines focusing on being more positive in the face of rejection—being resilient. Since Maddy had been less and less inclined to open any of her books, she tried to focus on what she was sure was a computer-generated quote and find a way to make her life better for adopting it.

So far, she'd been less than one hundred percent successful, but the act of focusing on the mantra made her more aware of her mental state. It also reminded her to get busy doing something besides painting. Painting gave her joy, was often an exercise in frustration, and gave her a place to disappear. What painting didn't help with was cardio. It didn't burn quite the calories it used to, either. And damn if her jeans weren't shrinking in the closet. Trying to be a whole person who didn't obsess over her relationship with her daughter, and wallow while dunking Oreos in milk for dinner, was hard work. Some days it was easier to Tweet at artist friends she'd never actually met.

Time to start living outside the canvas and social media.

With hope in her heart, Maddy opened the screen to her positive thought for the day.

Before she could read what her computer screen chose to reveal, General jumped into her lap, causing her to spill a bit of her tea. Thankfully, not all over her keyboard. It was always a risk having a cup filled to the brim with General in the house. "Thanks a lot, buddy," Maddy said, pulling her dog closer to her chest. She mopped up the spill with the folded paper towel she always kept on her desk as a make-shift coaster. "Your timing is impeccable as always. Shall we see what greatness the universe has in store for us today?"

General tilted his head and smiled that Westie smile at her, brown eyes glistening with what Maddy could only describe as mirth.

"I'll take that as a yes." Maddy took a big sip of her tea before General could help her spill it again, then she tapped the blinking icon which would set her day in motion. It read: *Three things cannot hide for long: the Moon, the Sun, and the Truth ~ Buddha.*

Maddy turned her head and spat a mouthful of tea onto the floor. She was really beginning to dislike Buddha.

She held General up so she could look the little man in the eye, as if it was his fault her stars weren't aligning the way she wanted. "Was it too much to ask for one date before the truth had taken away whatever calm I've built?"

Another head tilt was General's reply. Not finding that response particularly helpful, Maddy set him on the floor. One paw hit the tea she'd unceremoniously spat out. He shook his paw disdainfully before he trotted into the kitchen to pick at his breakfast. "Way to stick by my side when the going gets tough," Maddy called after him.

General ignored her.

"Thanks for nothing." Maddy hit the delete button. She didn't want to see that bit of Buddha's wisdom again.

You're the one who wanted to shake up your settled life. Put on your big-girl pants and prepare to be shaken. Be brave, it's going to be a bumpy ride.

Introspection, Maddy decided, was vastly overrated and dangerously under feared.

. . .

"Whatever you do, don't tell her the truth."

Drew knew it was a mistake to tell his father about his date with Maddy the second the words were out his mouth. That was a good three minutes ago, and J.T. hadn't stopped reciting bits of his home-brewed parental wisdom since. Each statement was more ridiculous than the last. One would think J.T. was a world-renowned expert on the fine art of dating by the way he was prattling on.

On the plus side, Drew hadn't seen J.T. this animated since J.T. won a date with a young country music star who'd taken the country by storm when she appeared on one of those *America's Got Talent* knock-off shows. J.T. was lucky that way. Send in a three-sentence paragraph on why you should win a date with a twenty-something rising country star, and shazam! —J.T. wins. As far as Drew knew, his father still had the occasional dinner with the woman, and she sent tickets and backstage passes to J.T. whenever she came to Milwaukee or Chicago. Apparently, his father charmed women of every age. Not romantically. J.T. hadn't seriously dated in years. He did seem to relate to the female population, though. Women loved him. Drew thought that probably had something to do with the fact that J.T. looked like a fit Santa Claus, and he was easy to talk to. The women of Fish Creek and beyond seemed to connect with that.

That didn't mean Drew had to listen to J.T. wax poetic on dubious dating advice. He did have work to do before he met Maddy for dinner. So far, J.T. hadn't made any kind of sense. What did he need to know to take a woman to dinner? He'd managed more than a few dinner dates in his life. Some of them even ended in a mutually agreeable fashion, even if they didn't lead to a second dinner date.

Dinner.

Dinner with Maddy was so much more than just dinner. It was the first step to having Maddy in his life again.

J.T. was still talking, but Drew had tuned him out. So he cleared his throat and went back to the last thing he could remember his well-meaning father saying. He addressed that, hoping it would get J.T. to shut up and let him get back to work. "Honesty kind of comes with the job description, Dad. As chief of police, I'm kind of expected to be honest." Drew shrugged, palms up, thinking he needed to state the obvious since his dad was on a roll. "I've also had some pretty negative experiences being less than truthful with women about my motives. I'm not going to make that mistake with Maddy. We're in a delicate spot right now, and I don't want to blow it before whatever *it* is gets started."

J.T. stopped talking mid-sentence. He leaned over Drew's desk, his eyes narrowed and serious. He was no longer the teasing father, he was the sincerely worried father. "Don't screw this up by telling Maddy the truth. There'll be time enough for that after she agrees to marry you. Better yet, wait until you've been married a decade or so. That ought to do it. You two have been dancing on egg shells with one another long enough. Eat the omelet already. Worry about how the eggs got broken ... well, *never* would be too soon for that."

When J.T. got this invested, it was best to pretend to take what he was saying seriously, no matter how insane it sounded.

Drew put down the pencil he'd been spinning between his fingers since before his father walked into his office. It was a habit he'd picked up long ago when he needed to focus on boring paperwork and not his lack-luster love life. Leave it to Maxie to tell everyone he had a date. Small town news spread faster than pink-eye through the local daycare. It seemed his romantic life was everyone's business, including his father's. "OK, Dad. I'll bite. Just what *truth* don't you want me to tell Maddy?"

"Well you can start with *not* telling her that you know that girl of hers is yours. You can follow that with *not* telling her you've known since you saw that heart-shaped birthmark on the girl's wrist."

J.T. held up a hand, effectively stopping whatever it was Drew was going to say. Since Drew didn't have much to say about that, he wisely shut his mouth and sat back in his chair. J.T. wasn't done and Drew was about out of secrets, so he waited for his dad to reveal something about Drew's private life Drew didn't know.

Plus, J.T. spoke with far more empathy than Drew had seen him display since he'd torn his rotator cuff and his ACL in the same career-ending season. Professional baseball ended for him then. Somehow this was far worse. These secrets could be the end of his second chance with the only woman Drew had truly loved. They could also end his attempt at fatherhood before he'd even had the time to figure out how to go about starting it.

"You should probably *not* tell Maddy you took out a second mortgage to buy-out her first big show. That just might kill all the confidence she's rightfully earned since."

As far as Drew's sins went, that was the least sinful in his mind. But now that J.T. had sowed the seeds of doubt about that, he wasn't going to be bringing it up. For all Drew knew, that would be one sin too many after the first two. He hadn't thought so then. He didn't think so now. But how was he supposed to know what would turn Maddy away from him?

Drew's biggest sin was his most embarrassing—he'd known where she was, he'd known how well she'd been doing in New York, and he'd turned away and came back to Fish Creek. He felt unworthy. He hadn't even bothered to give her a chance to prove him wrong. He just gave up. *That* was his biggest sin. Walking away from his own chance at happiness.

Well not again. Never again. Maddy would either give him a shot or not. One way or another, at least he'd get her out of his system. Who was he kidding? Drew thought. In twenty plus years, he'd yet to get Maddy Grace out of his system. Sometimes the people we love stick with us whether we want them to or not. That was the reality for Drew. He had to try. He had more to lose if he didn't.

Drew got up from his desk, walked around it, and

hugged his father. "I don't care how you knew about all that, old man. Just please keep it all to yourself as I try to figure out what to do next."

J.T. pounded his son's back and pulled away.

"Whatever you do, make sure you give it your best shot. Try not to stand in your way."

Drew wasn't sure he understood what J.T. meant by standing in his own way, but he'd sabotaged himself more than once. "I'll do what I can. Now get out of here and stop worrying. You've done your parental duty." Drew tapped at the paperwork on his desk. "I need to focus on these thefts down at the marina." Lord knew he had to focus on something he could actually do something about before he drove himself mad thinking about dinner with Maddy.

Had he known that catching the thief would mean the beginning of the end of his calm, settled life, he might have focused instead on whether to wear his new linen blazer with jeans or khakis. Tie or no tie? That kind of thinking would have kept his life on track.

Doing his job would lead to far more complications for decades to come.

CHAPTER NINE

Maddy added a swath of deep cerulean blue to the water in the foreground of her painting. She generally added images of people she knew who had passed, or people she loved or found interesting to her paintings. She did this in sketch form as if they were ghosts or spirits barely manifesting on the canvas. Just a tease, she thought, to let the viewer know there was a vision just outside the realm of reality that was no less real because it lived in the heart.

She sat on her favorite folding chair, gazing first at the marina filled with boats of all colors and sizes, then to her canvas, then back again. Maddy loved this time of year when the air was still warm during the day, but hints of fall's crispness crept into the evenings. She especially loved the crystal-clear evenings after bright warm days. There was always so much promise in the air. And the water changed hue with each passing cloud as the sun sank further in the sky.

Maddy was pleased with what she'd accomplished so

far. She had the basic outline of her marina scene. Most of the boats she chose to paint had been in harbor all week, so that was a plus for continuity. It seemed to Maddy that the owners of the boats were rarely in Fish Creek during the week. Some were. Some she'd come to know. Those were the owners who chose to live on their boats for much of the summer. Maddy thought that kind of life must be wildly romantic. Like old-time pirates with new-age toilets, showers, and refrigerators. That, she decided, would be her, once she sold enough paintings to justify a tiny water home she could only use three months out of the year.

Maybe she should think about getting a motorcycle first. She didn't know much about boats or motorcycles, but she did know motorcycles were less expensive, and she could take a motorcycle to the grocery store. She could also walk to the store since she lived right down the block, but that took all the danger out of the journey. What fun was that? she thought grinning. She was already learning how to tap dance, how much more danger did one middle-aged woman need in her life?

More than that, Madelyn Grace. Far more than that.

Maddy shook her head at her own foolishness as a quick flash of color caught her eye. A woman ... no, a girl scampered across the street at the end of the curve, hid for a moment behind a large oak tree, then jumped onto one of the boats that had been docked for at least the last week. Maddy didn't think it was occupied. She'd been at the marina working on this painting every afternoon for the last ten days, and she hadn't seen anyone come or go in that time. In fact, she was fairly certain the owners were in

Chicago getting ready for their son's wedding in Scotland at the end of September.

Maddy wasn't sure what made her put her brush down and set her easel aside. Before she knew what she was doing, she was up and walking toward the boat. She stopped at the dock to read the sign: "Owners only beyond this point." Maddy ignored it and walked up to the boat.

"Hello," she said softly.

No response.

"Hello," she said again, this time more loudly.

Nothing.

"I know you're in there. I saw you run from across the street."

A small face, streaked with dirt on the left side peeked out at Maddy from behind the edge on the stair leading to the living quarters. The girl was beautiful despite her unkempt appearance. She looked to be about sixteen or seventeen and way too skinny. Blonde, blue-eyed, and rosy-cheeked. She seemed to catch herself shrinking away because she stood straight, came up on deck, and stiffly held out her hand toward Maddy. "I'm Rose." She paused, seemed to think about what she'd said and added, "Rose Kelly."

Maddy took Rose's outstretched hand and shook it. Rose was stronger than she appeared and taller than Maddy estimated now that she was standing on deck, ram-rod straight, head held high. There was something special about this girl. Something brave and vulnerable and just out of Maddy's periphery. She didn't know why, but she was sure this girl needed help. She was also sure if she offered it, she'd never see Rose again.

"Madelyn Grace," Maddy said, finishing the handshake before letting Rose go. "But you can call me Maddy." Maddy shrugged wondering why she felt the need to blush at the use of her childhood name. She hadn't actually given anyone permission to use the shortened version of her name. Everyone in Fish Creek just seemed to assume they could, and they should since that's what she was called as a girl. "Everyone here seems to prefer Maddy to Madelyn."

"Madelyn is a lovely name. Melodic, even, when you say it right," Rose said, surprising her.

Odd choice of words for a girl who looked like she should be in high school, sneaking cigarettes or kisses under the bleachers. "How old are you?" Maddy asked.

Rose lost her small smile as she became more guarded. She didn't shrink back or run or defiantly raise her slightly pointed chin, but she did get a wary look in her eye. "Eighteen. How old are you?"

Bravo, Maddy thought. She'd deserved that. There was a small quiver of Rose's bottom lip when she asked the question, she knew to be rude. It was almost as if she was gearing up to be struck. The thought of anyone hitting Rose made Maddy's stomach turn. It also made every protective instinct in her light up like a Roman candle.

Maddy took a deep breath, checked her maternal feelings, and tried to smile in a way that would make Rose not want to run for the hills. In that moment, Maddy knew Rose had no business being on the Mackenzies' boat. She also knew the Mackenzies were insured, entitled, and wouldn't much miss their boat if it went up in flames.

They'd simply buy a newer, flasher, bigger one to replace it.

Maddy said, "I'm forty-four, Rose Kelly, and some days I feel like I'm sixty-four. Not today, though. Today I feel about twenty-five. I'm ready for a grand adventure. And I'm also very pleased to meet you."

The moment the words were out of Maddy's mouth, Maddy could see that Rose Kelly understood Maddy wasn't going to turn her in for squatting on the Mackenzie boat or anything else Rose might have done.

Rose let out a slow breath and seemed to relax, which made Maddy smile from her heart. Maddy wasn't like her artist friends. She didn't have the traditional artist's anything-goes kind of attitude. She was solid and staid and settled in a conservative, follow-the-rules kind of way. Not in this. Not today. Today she was making a new friend who looked like she needed solace and to rest for a bit.

Maddy looked at Rose's ill-fitting clothing. "Since you're obviously a guest of the Mackenzies', you might want to check out Bonnie Mackenzie's wardrobe. Bonnie is a little taller than you are, but otherwise, her cloths should be a good fit. Oh, and I'm pretty sure Bonnie and Max keep an assortment of frozen meals from the White Gull's chef in the freezer. No telling how long they've been there and the Mackenzies won't be back until the end of the season—sometime in early October—since they're traveling to Scotland for a month for their son's wedding."

Maddy feigned an affected British accent. "Apparently, all the right people will be attending. The event of the season for Highland society, I'm told. Even Nicola Sturgeon will be there, because the Mackenzies just had to invite her."

Rose laughed, as Maddy hoped she would.

Maddy smiled and said, "I paint here every afternoon." She pointed toward the grassy clearing under the willow tree where she'd left her canvas and paints. "Maybe we could have lunch together one of these afternoons if you're not too busy."

Rose nodded once, shy now that she didn't have to defend herself. "Maybe. I'd like that."

"Great. It's a date, Rose Kelly."

Maddy turned and walked away before she frightened her new friend away.

The sun was reflecting off the water, making it hard to read Rose's expression as Maddy turned back to wave.

Rose lifted a hand, then quickly disappeared below deck again as if she'd never really been there at all.

Maddy pulled a new brush out of her leather travel kit, one with fine bristles that would help her create fine lines, and she started to add spirit to her painting. Outlined in brown, filled in with swatches of light yellow, rose, blue, and cream, a form took shape.

A young girl, sweetly smiling with eyes older than her years and with a secret she wouldn't be telling, sat on the deck of the last boat in the long line of boats Maddy painted. Some of the boats had names. Some didn't. Maddy named this boat: KELLY ROSE.

Maddy heard the rustling of grass behind her.

She ignored it, intent on finishing what was flowing through her onto the canvas while she still had the soft glow of waning summer light.

A throat cleared behind her. She had no way of knowing how much time had passed after the rustling settled down. Then came his voice, low, throaty, and filled with admiration, "Wow, Maddy. I know you don't like anyone to view your work before it's done, but this is spectacular."

Drew's softly uttered praise drew her out of her work and back into the real world. For the first time, she noticed the sun was setting. How long had she been out here? Maddy looked at her watch. *7:42.* She whirled around without settling her brush down and splattered brown paint across the front of what looked to be a brand new white linen jacket.

Maddy looked up at Drew, horrified.

He didn't even notice. He was too preoccupied looking over her shoulder at her painting. "Who are the girls?" he asked. "The older one looks familiar somehow, but I can't place her."

Maddy turned back to her painting, noticing for the first time the detail she'd put into the girl's postures and facial expressions as they played tea with what had been Aunt Ruby's tea set until she'd accidently broken it. Maddy didn't realize she'd painted Julie when she was about five— that magical age, right before Julie discovered there was a world outside of her mother. A big world filled with adventures that didn't include Maddy.

Maddy pointed toward the ephemeral image of her daughter and said, "That's Julie when she was about five. I saved all my tips to buy her that dress for her first day of kindergarten. I'd forgotten about that dress. I can't imagine why I painted it now."

Drew looked from the canvas to Maddy's face, scrutinizing, searching for something Maddy couldn't identify. It was like he was looking directly into her heart searching for the girl he once knew, or the woman she was now. Maddy wasn't sure. As she looked at her rapidly drying canvas, she wasn't sure of much of anything that happened today.

Drew's eyes narrowed. "And the other girl, the one serving the tea, who is she?"

Maddy didn't know why she felt she needed to keep Rose Kelly a secret, but she felt it deeply, so she trusted herself. "She's a figment of my imagination. I created her from thin air." Maddy smiled to cover her nervousness in the face of Drew's intent gaze. "And paint." Maddy turned away from his knowing eyes and back to Rose's image. "She's beautiful, though, isn't she?"

Maddy felt Drew's eyes on her, warm and familiar, yet shades different from the heat she'd felt from him as a teenager. Deeper. More certain. Dangerous. "Yes, *she* is," he said, smiling at her.

Flustered, and frustrated because of it, Maddy jumped up too quickly from her chair and hit him again with her brush. This time catching his bright blue shirt.

Drew captured her wrist and gently took the brush from her hand. Then he smiled at her ruefully and all the tension she'd been feeling seconds before washed away. "I guess I'm going to have to have you paint the rest of my jacket, just so I don't look like an idiot who walked into a brush."

Maddy took the brush from him, wiped it off, and put it away. "I'm sorry. I lost track of time." Maddy looked into Drew's face, marveling at the subtle changes the years had wrought. Fine lines crinkled around his eyes and mouth. His face was leaner, tanner, more masculine than it was when they were in school. He looked like he worried more now, judging by the frown lines on his forehead. His light-brown hair shone with gold in fading sun. "You certainly are a handsome man, Drew Selleck," Maddy said, leaning into him.

Drew cupped her face in both hands, thumbs grazing her cheekbones gently. "And you, Maddy Grace, are about the most beautiful thing I have ever seen." He smiled slowly. "Even with paint on your temples and ratty old sneakers on your toes."

Maddy's eyes flared as she jerked her head to her feet. She was indeed wearing her rattiest pair of what had once been neon-green canvas Converse high-tops. They were faded and torn now, and perfect for painting. Hardly perfect for dining.

"Oh, God, I've ruined dinner, haven't I?"

Drew shook his head and held out his hand. "Not even close. I called Serendipity and changed our reservation to 8:30. You still have time to shower and change if you want. Or we could go as a mismatched painted pair. Your choice."

Maddy made short work of packing up her supplies and loading them into her bag. She'd walked to the marina, so she asked Drew to give her a ride home so she could change.

"Definitely," he said as he led her to the passenger side of his Jeep, hand at the small of her back. "I did as instructed and ordered two bottles of pinot noir. One for you, and after I have a glass out of the second, the rest is all yours."

"Trying to get me knockered and have your wicked way with me?" Maddy asked, feeling light-hearted enough to tease him in a way adults with everything to lose shouldn't tease.

"Nope. When I have my wicked way with you, Madelyn Grace, all your faculties will be in prime working order." His voice deepened and became more intimate, "and I hope you will be having more wickedness with me then you've had before."

Maddy didn't say another word on the short drive to her condo. Which was wise because she was beginning to love all iterations of the word *wicked* far more than she should.

CHAPTER TEN

The restaurant Serendipity had been named Trio the last time Maddy visited Fish Creek. When it was Trio, it served Tuscan food, delicious and well-prepared. The owners of Serendipity had changed the mango-hued walls, graced with fields of lavender and Italian country-scapes, to soft blue-grey that matched the horizon at sunset, where water from lake Michigan touched the sky. It was, to use Rose Kelly's word, lovely. No flamboyant landscapes. Just simple color, clear glass, and rich naturally-stained wood. A small gas fireplace surrounded by glass sat inside a dividing wall, clearly visible from each side of the restaurant. Orange and yellow and bright-blue flames danced from the fireplace's river rock. The tables were covered in butcher's paper. The place settings were mismatched but elegant. The light fixtures mimicked the effect of candlelight throughout.

Serendipity was simple, elegant, and far more romantic than any other restaurant Maddy had been to in the entirety of the Door peninsula. And every table in the place was filled.

Drew nodded at people, but kept moving. Again, his gentle but firm hand pressed the small of Maddy's back as the host led them to a table in the corner. A bottle of pinot noir sat upright on the table, opened to breathe. Another reclined in a silver bucket, wrapped in a black cloth napkin.

Drew held out her chair for her, the chair with its back to the other diners. She would face him and the floor-to-ceiling windows that showcased a tiny outdoor garden complete with a lit waterfall. Drew settled himself without a word, but Maddy could see that if he wanted to, he could scan the entire room without straining himself. Both exits and the door to the kitchen included.

The tall host was handsome in the way most athletic men in their early twenties were handsome. He had a haircut that was severely cut in the back and rakishly hung over one eye in the front. It made Maddy want to find a scissors and cut it. She was far older, she decided, than her inner twenty-five-year-old who'd come out to play earlier in the day. *That* Maddy should have been all over this host, especially after he winked at her and asked, "Shall I pour, Chief Selleck?"

Drew looked at her like he knew what she was thinking and said, "Pour for the lady first, Derrik. We'll see if it meets her expectations."

Without looking up at Derrik, Maddy said, "Fill the glass, Derrik. Then fill the chief's. Unless the chief would like to *sample* my wine on his jacket. He hasn't had quite enough color yet today."

Drew grinned and raised an eyebrow at her. "Do that

and I'll throw you over my shoulder, grab that unopened bottle, and head straight out the front door. All of Fish Creek will know the details of our *dinner* before I get you home."

The glint in his eye told Maddy he'd do it.

"Always had to rise to the challenge and go one better. That hasn't changed," Maddy said. She lifted her glass, slowly swirled its contents, inhaled, then took a small sip. It was delicious, smooth, full, and potent without heavy lingering. She looked up at Derrik. "It's perfect," she said, meaning it.

Derrik listed the specials, handed Maddy and Drew each a menu, and left.

Their server appeared soon after, bringing rosemary herb butter and some of the best warm bread Maddy had ever had. The menu was short and since Maddy no longer ate meat, her options were rather limited. She did eat seafood, so she ordered the salmon with asparagus and wild thyme baby potatoes.

Drew ordered a fillet. Rare. Somethings didn't change. Some did. Dramatically.

After the server left, Drew looked at her and said, "Finish your wine. Because we've got a lot to talk about before our food arrives, and you're going to need it."

There were many things Drew wanted to talk to Maddy about. Why did she leave? He was relatively certain his mother had something to do with that, and his unrelenting desire to be a star. Why didn't she tell him about Julie? That undoubtedly also had more to do with his being drafted into the major leagues before he finished his first semester at the University of Wisconsin. What did she want from him now? Did she want him as much as he wanted to build a life with her? Would she fight his need to make himself known to Julie? The better question was whether he'd allow her to have any say in the matter at all. She had kept Julie from him. Whatever her rationale for that and whatever blame she laid at his feet, none of it justified keeping him from his adult daughter—a daughter he wanted to know and wanted a chance to love.

All these questions ran through his mind at the speed of lightning, cracking the sky in the summer storms out on the bay. Hard. Fast. Violent. Then gone.

What he said as the silence mounted was, "Dance with me. Give me two classes a week until the Thanksgiving Gala to get to know me again as I get to know you. All the funds go to finding a cure for Alzheimer's. It's a good cause. *I'm* a good cause. Come dance with me, Maddy. What do you have to lose?"

Whatever her reply would have been was stymied by the arrival of their food.

. . .

They made small talk after that. Little teasing. Lots of safe questions about work and family, what movies they enjoyed, what they each liked to read. It struck Maddy as funny and sweet that Drew actually enjoyed romance novels as much as he liked spy novels. She didn't believe him at first, until he hit her with the characters from Cathy Maxwell's Scottish historical novels and Diana Gabaldon's

Outlander books. As for the *Outlander* series, he said Claire should just make a choice already and stick with it. But he did like author Susan Elizabeth Phillips. The last one really surprised Maddy. She'd read a few of those books. They were funny and more than a little sexy. Drew liked the stories with the Chicago Stars the best. Well, that made sense to her. He had been a professional athlete, no matter how briefly. Drew also read Thomas Paine, John Donahue, and everything James Lee Burke ever wrote. The man was an enigma, and far deeper than she'd given him credit for.

Die Hard was his second favorite Christmas movie, so he did have his flaws, but she could hardly fault him for loving a movie that made her smile.

"So, what's your favorite Christmas movie?" Maddy asked finishing her third glass of wine as their server delivered the dessert menu.

"*How the Grinch stole Christmas.*"

Maddy almost spat out her wine.

"So, you still can't swallow when your brain tells you to laugh. Interesting." Drew lifted his napkin and dabbed at the corner of her mouth. She hadn't felt any wine leave her mouth, but she sure felt that touch. All the way to her toes. She felt hot all over when he pulled his hand away. His eyes lingering on her lips didn't help.

Sensing she should leave, the server put the menus on the table and turned away.

"You're kidding about the Grinch, right? Please tell me you're not talking about the Jim Carey version."

Drew shuddered dramatically. "Nope. Animated for me, all the way. Carey's just creepy."

"Agreed."

"Don't tell me your favorite Christmas movie. Let me guess." Drew looked at her critically and cocked his head just like General did. Maddy couldn't help it, the image made her laugh.

"I love it when you laugh. Your whole face lights up, and I just want to laugh right along with you." He did love her laugh. It did weird things to him. It made him smile. It made him want to hold her. It made him want to see her doing it naked.

Her face flashed her embarrassment, which struck Drew as odd. They were adults. They'd kissed before. They'd made love before, more times than he could count. But that was when Maddy thought they'd marry and have children after college. Before he left to become the next Robin Yount. Young, ambitious, and wicked good—just like Rock'n Robin, only faster. Drew was going to have to take it slow with Maddy. He wanted to hear her laugh again. He wanted to hear her laugh with him for the rest of his life. He could keep his desires to himself for now.

"Let me guess. A woman who doesn't appreciate the Christmas magic that is magnificently portrayed in *Die Hard*, probably gets teary-eyed on the twentieth rerun of *Love Actually*."

Maddy choked. Thankfully she was drinking water, so what little she had to cough into her napkin was clear.

Drew groaned as he squeezed his eyes shut and dropped his head to his chest in defeat. "Come on, Maddy. The best part of the movie is the airport scenes with normal people. The kid is the only character besides the aging rock star worth a damn. Please tell me that's not your go-to movie."

She shot him an evil grin. "Yep. Every year. I even watch it in July, just so I can gear up. On my third DVD, because I wore out the first two."

Drew held a finger to his head and pretended to shoot. "Hopeless. Utterly hopeless."

"Says the man who still watches cartoons."

"Animated movies."

"Yeah, right. So much more mature."

"Shut up and order dessert."

Maddy looked at the three-item menu and frowned. "Everything has cherries."

Drew looked at her dumbfounded. He'd forgotten her aversion to cherries. "How can you be born and raised in the Door and hate cherries?"

"I don't hate cherries. I just don't like them mixed with everything." Maddy was mumbling. Apparently, this was a sore spot for her. Maddy had never been able to tell Ruby she disliked cherries. Ruby put cherries in everything she baked. And the woman baked frequently—cherry pie, cherry turnover, and cherry coffee cake.

"Ruby bringing over bakery again?" Drew asked.

Maddy put down her menu. "This morning she brought cherry kringle. I didn't think it was possible to hate kringle. I was wrong."

"Want to get out of here?"

"Badly."

"Should I take the wine to go?"

"Next time," Maddy said.

"I'll hold you to that."

Drew paid the bill in cash and ushered Maddy out of the restaurant before their server could ask about coffee or dessert.

All eyes were on them as they left.

Dinner with the chief of police in a small town was tantamount to acknowledging an illicit affair, or announcing an engagement, depending on the age, gender, and gossip quotient of the observer. Add a romantic history, and what got whispered grew more conspiratorial and grandiose.

It was just dinner, for heaven's sake.

CHAPTER ELEVEN

"I'm telling you, Maxie, it was more than just dinner. Our chief is in love." MaryEllen Loomis was one of Maxie's part-time dance instructors. She was young, graceful, a great dancer, and a decent instructor. What MaryEllen wasn't was discreet, overly intellectual, or quiet.

"They're friends, MaryEllen. They've also known each other since grade school. Why wouldn't they go out to eat together? Don't read more into it than that."

"Well the chief was holding her face. Apparently feeding some sort of cherry dessert too. Oh, and they drank two bottles of wine. *Two.* That woman is driving our chief to drink." MaryEllen shook her head. "This can't be good, Maxie. Everyone knows Drew isn't a drinker."

"Actually, Drew likes beer," said Maddy as she walked from the back of the dance studio to the front. "Craft beer more than name brand. He also enjoys dry red wine and the occasional bourbon straight up. However, you are correct. Drew rarely drinks alcohol out, so I could be to blame for that." Maddy nodded with what she hoped was appropriate introspection. Then she added, "Come to think of it, I *am* to blame for that bit of Drew Selleck's fall into depravity. I did insist on two bottles of pinot. I insisted on lobster and oysters on the half-shell too, but apparently Alexander's is closed for the season. Something to do with renovations to the kitchen. So, I had to make due with *two* bottles of wine at Serendipity. I can almost hear the gates of hell opening for me as we speak."

Maxie was smiling ear to ear as Maddy spoke, one hand curved around her narrow hip. Casually sensual. It was as if the woman couldn't help exuding sexual promise, even when she wasn't trying. And I'm the devil's temptress, Maddy thought. How absurdly ironic.

She really didn't know why she baited a woman she'd never met, but the gossip reminded her of why she left Fish Creek in the first place—third parties who had no business opining about her personal business.

The sleigh bells on Maxie's door chimed behind Maddy, but she didn't even turn to look. "You are wrong about one thing," Maddy told MaryEllen. "Drew still owes me dessert."

Then Maddy felt the warm palm on her shoulder and within milliseconds Drew's scent assailed her. Warm and green and woodsy, as if he'd been chopping wood and cutting grass at the same time. He bent to kiss her cheek and said, "And I'll be paying that dessert debt tonight if you're free."

MaryEllen stared at Drew, mouth open, hand on her chest as if she were clutching at invisible pearls.

Maddy refused to blush. That kiss, no matter how

platonically given, shook her. She was sure that display of gentlemanly affection was for the benefit of the woman standing next to Maxie. Judging by Maxie's knowing glance and slight smirk, she wasn't buying the old-friend-on-the-way-to-something-more-intimate routine. Unfortunately for Maddy, she was buying it. Hook, line, and sinker.

"Ruby told me you'd be here this morning," Drew said.

"When did you have time to talk to Ruby?" Maddy asked.

"I spoke with her yesterday afternoon when she delivered cherry coffee cake to the office. She'd just got done delivering your kringle. She had that naughty look on her face when she casually told me about your tap dance lessons. You know she's yanking your chain with all the baking, right? She's known since you were a kid you don't like cooked cherries, or any cherries not served in a bowl with the stems on and the pits still in."

"Thanks a lot, Drew Selleck," Ruby said, walking through the door. Usually, Maddy would have picked Ruby up, but this morning Ruby called and said she had to run an errand and would meet Maddy at the dance studio. "I've been waiting for Madelyn to stand up and let her desires be known for years. Now you've gone and blown it. She doesn't have to say what pleases her now that you've let the cat out of the bag."

Maddy's eyes narrowed as she took in her unrepentant aunt.

Drew walked over and gave Ruby a quick hug. "Morning, Ruby. Dad's been asking about you."

"I see J.T. every day. All that man has to do is look to

know how I'm doing."

"You know Dad. Always has to be kept up to date on the women in his life," Drew said conspiratorially.

Ruby slapped his shoulder with little force and deep affection. "You're as big a flirt as your father, Drew Selleck, and an even bigger tattletale."

"Yes, ma'am. And twice as handsome."

Ruby made a rude noise and hit Drew again, this time more forcefully. "Not on your best day."

Drew put a hand to his heart. "You wound me, Ruby."

Ruby squinted up at him. "Now that you've seen my niece, don't you have work to do?"

Drew sobered. "I do." Drew turned to Maddy. "That's actually why I'm here. I need to talk to you about a"—he looked up and saw Maxie and MaryEllen leaning in to hear every word—"About a case I'm working on. I need you to stop by the office when you're finished here. Shouldn't take long, but I do need to speak with you."

Maddy frowned. "Officially?"

Drew nodded, with a seriousness in his eyes. "Officially," he confirmed.

Then he dismissed her and turned to Maxie. "Maddy has agreed to partner with me to do a number for the gala. We need to schedule lessons twice a week."

Maxie went to the desk and pulled up her calendar for private lessons. "Salsa?" she asked.

Drew glanced back at Maddy, his expression as unreadable as it had been when he told her he needed to see her in his official capacity as chief of police. "No, ballroom dance."

"Waltz?" Maxie asked.

Drew looked over his shoulder at Maddy again. A slow smile graced his handsome face as a sensual haze hooded his eyes. "Make it rumba, Maxie," he said, turning back to her.

Maxie typed furiously, surveying her computer screen with the intensity and focus of a teenaged gamer.

"MaryEllen isn't teaching ballroom, is she?" Drew asked, nodding toward the woman.

Maxie didn't look up from her screen. "No, MaryEllen is taking over the children's classes. Peter will be teaching ballroom dance. So far, though, you and Maddy are the only ones signed up." Maxie looked up from her screen at Maddy. "How does Tuesdays and Thursdays at seven work for you?"

Since her best light came before seven, Maddy's evenings were free. "Tuesdays and Thursdays should work fine." What in the world had she just gotten herself into? Ballroom dance? When in the world was she going to need Ballroom dance?

When you dance at your daughter's wedding.

Well there was that.

Drew finished up with Maxie, handing her his credit card. Maddy had forgotten. Agreeing to dance lessons meant someone had to pay for the privilege. She had meant to bring up the cost with Drew. She didn't want to pay for all of it, but she would pay her half. Before she could say anything, Drew said, "Don't forget, Maddy. My office. As soon as you and Ruby are finished."

He was out the door in full chief of police mode

before she could ask what rumba was.

. . .

Ruby made it through dance class, but just barely. Tap dance was far harder than it looked. Her joints ached. Her stomach turned. And every muscle she had that still had some fight in it, was bone-deep sore.

"Are you sure I can't take you on your errand?" Maddy asked her as they sat on a black velvet couch, changing back into their street shoes. "You look tired, Ruby."

"Drew needs you at the station."

"Drew can wait."

Ruby smiled at that. One thing Maddy was and would always be, was over protective of Ruby. It was as if Maddy thought she owed Ruby more than love and kindness, a deeper debt she could never repay. It wasn't like that at all. Maddy owed her nothing, but the woman Maddy had become was very much like the little girl she'd been—loyal, loving, and fiercely protective of those she thought God would take from her sooner than she was ready to let them go.

God had taken her parents. Surely if she did the least thing wrong, he'd take Ruby too. That was how Maddy saw things as a child. Ruby had worked hard to dispel that kind of thinking in Maddy, but it hadn't worked. Not really. Maddy still held on too close. Maddy was still far too sentimental in her attachments. Ruby needed her to focus on making herself complete without making her life revolve around Ruby and Julie. They were both going to disappoint her. Ruby by dying. Julie by never being a little girl again.

It was time to push Maddy into realizing she could make her own happiness if she gave herself half a chance. "Drew cannot wait," Ruby said, pulling tight on the laces of her sneakers. The effort cost her. Today was not a good day. She needed to get away from Maddy and fast. "And I can run my own errands. I'm sixty-four, not 104."

That seemed to get Maddy to understand she didn't need to push. Ruby wasn't sure what was going through Maddy's mind when she held out her hand to help Ruby up. Her face got quiet and inscrutable, like she was hiding within, like she'd done right after her parents died.

After a time, Maddy seemed to formulate the words to express the emotion she couldn't quite define. It was in moments like these that Maddy was truly hidden from Ruby. "Why do you keep giving me cherry desserts when you've known all along I don't like them?"

Not what Ruby expected but a teaching moment nonetheless.

Ruby smiled and reached up to cup the side of Maddy's face. Such a lovely woman her niece had become, even more beautiful now than when she was child. And Madelyn Grace was the most beautiful child Ruby had ever seen. "Because, dear heart, I've been waiting for you to stand up and say what it is you do like and what you do want. Life isn't about avoiding what you don't want. It's about actively seeking what you do want."

Maddy scrunched up her face, then settled on a drawn-out frown before she smiled at Ruby. "You sound like one of my self-help books you keep pilfering."

Ruby tamped down her need to pull Maddy close and tell her everything in her life was going to be all right. It wouldn't be. Especially when she would find out Ruby was dying. "How would you know? You collect the things, but I've yet to see you actually read one."

Maddy walked her to the door. "I thumb through and read the occasional italicized quote." Maddy held the door open for her.

Ruby walked through, anxious to see Maddy gone now that her strength was rapidly fading.

"At least you didn't say, 'Life's a bowl of cherries,'" said Maddy.

Ruby looked at her without cracking a smile. "Life *is* a bowl of cherries. That doesn't mean you have to eat them."

Maddy laughed.

"Go," Ruby said, shooing her niece along. "You've got a handsome man with the power to lock you up for keeping him waiting."

Maddy leaned down and kissed the top of Ruby's head. Then she was off, all but running toward her little white Lincoln. Ruby felt a rush of pride knowing Maddy would always be able to thrive on her own, tough as nails and just as jagged inside. Now all she needed was a little happily-ever-after, and Ruby's job at adoptive parenting would be complete.

Ruby fished her cell phone out of her bag and hit number two on her favorites. "J.T., I need you to come and get me. I'm sitting on the bench outside the dance studio."

"Be there in a minute," J.T. said, tossing down a ten on

the counter of Rooster's next to his half-eaten breakfast.

True to his word, J.T. pulled up in just over ninety seconds. He took one look at Ruby and said, "What's wrong?"

"I need you to take me to Julie's clinic."

CHAPTER TWELVE

"Let me get this straight," Julie said, eyeing everyone in the small examining room, starting with her great-aunt Ruby, whom she loved more than anyone in the world, to J.T. who seemed deeply worried about Ruby, to her assistant who seemed peacefully resigned amidst the chaos that had just descended upon her clinic. "The three of you thought it was a good idea to get high in my clinic at," Julie looked at her watch, "9:30 in the morning. On a weekday."

"No one thought it was a good idea, Doc," Peter said. "It was the only safe option available."

Ruby sucked in the smoke from an overly large joint that J.T. had rolled for her. This was unreal, thought Julie. The doctor part of her brain hadn't kicked into gear yet. She was still firing on great-grand-niece cylinders. "Does Mom know?" she asked, reeling from the fact she was now part of a criminal conspiracy to ingest an illegal substance.

"Of course not," Ruby said, exhaling. The effort to speak cost her, and she coughed. "And you're not going to tell her."

Ruby started coughing again, and J.T. Selleck, a man Julie had met only a handful of times, glared at her. "Stop judging and start doctoring," he said, yanking Julie out of her funk.

She looked at Ruby critically, seeing for the first time the pallor of her skin and the shrunken area beneath her eyes. She'd eaten lunch with Ruby yesterday. She hadn't looked this tired or this old then.

Ruby looked at J.T. and nodded toward the trash bin.

J.T. handed it to her.

Ruby heaved into it. The tortured sounds of her stomach revolting filled the small room. The sound, which produced nothing of value since Ruby had nothing in her stomach to expel, galvanized Julie. She pushed J.T. out of the way, lifted Ruby's chin and examined her eyes. Her pupils were dilated, but that was most likely due to the hash-laced marijuana.

Julie lifted Ruby's wrist, felt for her pulse, and counted.

"Your pulse is steady, your breathing is shallow, and you look a decade older than you did yesterday." Julie looked into Ruby's eyes, knowing what was wrong but demanding Ruby tell her anyway.

Ruby handed the joint to Peter who took a toke on it before tamping it out.

Julie glared at him. They'd discuss that later. In private.

Peter lifted his chin, exhaled, and shrugged. He wasn't the least bit worried about how Julie saw him. He did appear genuinely worried about Ruby. That saved him from most of Julie's ire.

"I've been diagnosed with stage four pancreatic

cancer," Ruby said.

That hit Julie like an arrow from a crossbow fired at close range. There was no recovering from that kind of shot—the arrow went straight through, killing before the victim knew he'd been hit. Just like pancreatic cancer hit, wreaking its damage before modern medicine could stop it.

"Chemo?" Julie asked.

"J.T. saw me through two courses of chemo already," Ruby said, smiling wanly at J.T. "There won't be a third".

Anger hit first, before denial, or bargaining. "So, what now? J.T. holds your hand, and Peter supplies your pot? When were you going to tell me?"

Peter handed Ruby back her marijuana. He also handed her a towel he dampened with cool water from the sink. "Actually, J.T. grows Ruby's pot. I just help her get by when J.T. isn't around. I also make brownies for her and sit with her when she needs me." Peter went back to the sink, got a paper cup from the metal dispenser next to it, and filled the cup. He handed the cup to Ruby who took it with a shaking hand. Then he turned and looked at Julie as if she were a recalcitrant child who'd just had a temper tantrum in the middle of a store. He was the disappointed, angry, and put-upon parent stuck with instructing her on acceptable behavior.

Actually, he looked like he wanted to put her over his knee and spank her, but that visual was doing nothing to calm Julie's already volatile mood, so she squashed it.

"I told Ruby to come in to see you weeks ago," said Peter. "That she's here now tells you all you need to know about how bad she feels. Do your job, Doc. Help her with her nausea, systemic weakness, and her pain."

Julie looked from Ruby to J.T. who was now stoically waiting for Julie to do something, anything, to help the woman he obviously loved. She thought she saw something else in J.T.'s intense gaze that was not directed solely at her ability to help medically, but Julie disregarded that. She had bigger things on her mind.

"How long," she asked Ruby.

Ruby shrugged. "You know doctors, pessimistic creatures, as a rule."

"How long, Aunt Ruby." It wasn't a question, it was a demand.

"I don't know, honey. Six months. Maybe a year."

"I'm going to need you to sign a release so I can review all your medical records."

"I've already got that," Peter said. "I sent for them a month ago." Peter pulled out a thumb drive and handed it to Julie. "They're all there, including the ones from when J.T. and I took Ruby to the Mayo Clinic."

Julie looked at Peter stunned. She nodded, understanding for the first time how serious Ruby's condition was and that she had relied on two men, not her family, to get her through what had to be the most monumental experience of her life. Julie quickly put together supplements that would ease the nausea Ruby was feeling and help her regain some of her energy. She also grabbed a few painkillers to supplement the herb Ruby had already chosen to lessen her pain.

Julie went to Ruby and spoke as if the men who'd seen to the intimate and illegal details of her care weren't in the room. "You have to tell Mom, Aunt Ruby."

"No," Ruby said lifting her chin. "Absolutely not. And you're not going to tell her either. Maddy is just starting to focus on what she wants in life again. I'm not going to let you or anyone else throw a wrench into that."

Julie sighed and shook her head. Ruby was her rock. She was the one Julie came to with every problem and every need and every gripe—most of which had been about her mother. Ruby listened, gave advice, and gently redirected. What Ruby didn't do was judge or demand. Well, she was demanding now, and Julie would abide by that demand. Not because she agreed with it, but because she loved and respected Ruby.

"What can I do to help?" Julie asked.

Ruby smiled at her and handed Julie her dance bag. "You can see if my tap shoes fit. If they don't, you'll be ordering a pair that do. You're now dancing with your mother."

Julie startled and retreated from the bag as if it held a pile of writhing snakes. "What am I supposed to tell her about why I'm taking your classes?"

"Take the bag, Julie," Peter said, using Julie's name for the first time since she hired him.

Julie took the bag.

"Tell her Ruby has arthritis in her ankles, and she can't take the pounding in her joints. That last bit is true as far as it goes," Peter said calmly. Always the pragmatist. Always filled with at least half-truths. Julie wanted to hit him. She also wanted to rage and howl at the moon. Neither of which she was going to let Ruby see her do. If Ruby could be strong, Julie could surely find her own backbone. She wasn't a quitter.

"She'll never believe I volunteered to dance with her," Julie said under her breath, surprising herself with the sadness in her voice.

"Make her believe," Ruby said as if it were that easy.

Peter said, "It can't be that hard to convince your mother you'd like to spend a few hours a week with her."

Wanna bet?

"What are the two of you dancing to?" Julie asked.

"*Uptown Funk You Up* by Bruno Mars," Ruby said smiling. "It's actually quite catchy. You'll like it."

Julie shook her head and found her first smile. She did like Bruno Mars, especially that song. The fact that she had anything so mundane and just plain weird in common with her oh-so-cultured mother seemed utterly ridiculous. Especially under these circumstances.

"Fine. I'll do it. But you have to promise me you'll tell Mom about your condition before she finds out on her own."

"I won't promise you that, Julie. There is no bargain to be made here. You'll either do what I'm asking or you won't."

"You are a stubborn old woman, you know that?" Julie took Ruby's tap shoes out of the pink box they were in, and she put the box back into the bag. She sat on her stool and tried on the shoes. They fit. Perfectly. "I'll dance, Ruby, but you better damn well make it to that gala."

"That," Ruby said, "Heaven can wait for. I wouldn't miss seeing my girls dance together for anything."

Julie waited to cry until J.T. had Ruby safely ensconced in his car.

"Go away, Peter," she said as Ruby and J.T. drove away.

Peter ignored her and pulled her into his chest and held her there while she cried instead.

. . .

J.T. looked over at Ruby where she rested in the passenger seat as he pulled to a stop in her drive. "How bad is it, Ruby?"

Ruby opened her eyes and smiled at him. "Bad enough."

She looked far better now than she had in Julie's examining room. "Not bad enough to keep you from dancing, though, is it?"

"No. I could probably have made it to the gala, but I'm not getting better, J.T., and it's getting harder and harder to maintain my strength."

J.T. sat back, content to sit in the car with Ruby and talk. "You manipulated your great-grandniece."

"You mean your granddaughter," Ruby countered. It was the first time either of them admitted the relationship openly.

J.T. squeezed Ruby's hand. "Yep, I mean my granddaughter. And you manipulated her but good. Aren't you ashamed of yourself?"

"Not in the least. If I waited for Julie and Maddy to bury the hatchet in their own time, I'd be dead long before they admitted there was a hatchet to begin with." Ruby looked at him and for the first time J.T. saw genuine worry in her gaze. "You aren't ashamed of me, are you, J.T.? I'm not sure I could bear that."

J.T. leaned over, unbuckled Ruby's seatbelt and lifted her meager weight into his lap. "Darling girl, as the song goes, I'll love you till the rivers all run dry. You'll have to try a hell of a lot harder to make me feel shame for anything I do for you. Including breaking the law."

Ruby rested her head on his shoulder. "I wish I had more time to try."

"Me too, Darlin. Me too."

CHAPTER THIRTEEN

The Gibraltar Police Department building was set back from the main road into and out of Fish Creek on what was otherwise a pedestrian walkway. It had a generous parking lot, considering the number of employees, and yet it looked almost residential in that it was surrounded by trees. It was probably the prettiest police building in the county. Certainly, it was no hardship coming to work from an aesthetic perspective, Drew thought. Even his office was pleasant with its large windows, open concept, and comfortable chairs.

The building itself wasn't scary or threatening or the least bit unnerving. Some of what happened within the walls, though, that could be very scary on occasion. Especially during tourist season when too much alcohol mixed with motorsports. Helping to extricate someone from twisted wreckage as Flight for Life hovered in, always turned Drew's stomach.

Today he wasn't preoccupied with the accidents that came with being a tourist hotspot. Today he was concerned with the thefts that where happening up and down the peninsula, primarily in Egg Harbor, Fish Creek, Ephraim, and Sister Bay—communities connected by one road in and one road out, communities that depended on the tourist trade for their livelihoods, communities that all had marinas.

Drew's deputy handed him the newest stack of incident reports detailing the latest burglaries.

"It's weird, Chief," said Sam. "If you take all the incidents and put them together, they don't emerge as the kind of pattern we usually see. Some of these burglaries, primarily the one's committed here in Fish Creek, aren't worth turning in to the insurance companies. There's so little actually taken and most of that has little value."

Drew poured himself a cup of coffee and sat down across from Sam's desk. His own office was set away from the lobby and the front door, and he wanted to keep an eye out for Maddy. Drew glanced at his watch. She was due to come by any minute now.

"What does that tell you?" Drew asked, knowing what it told him and hoping Sam was connecting the dots as rapidly.

"It tells me we're dealing with at least two perpetrators," Sam said.

Drew sipped his coffee, keeping one eye on the door. "Why?"

"Because a handful of these complaints report food and clothing stolen while cash, jewelry, and electronics—easily taken—were left behind."

Drew glanced at the door again.

"For Pete's sake, Drew, Maddy will get here when she gets here. She won't be blowing off the chief of police even if she'd blow off Drew Selleck, which I doubt she'd do, seeing how well your dinner went last night."

Drew dropped the foot he'd been resting on his knee to the floor and sat up in the chair. "Is there anyone who doesn't know I took Maddy to dinner last night?"

Sam grinned, then took a sip of his own coffee. "Doubt it. It was the main topic of conversation at the Rooster this morning."

"Great."

Just what he needed, Drew thought, everyone in town taking turns regaling Maddy with every romantic liaison he's had since his ex-wife left him for a center fielder who has long since moved on to trophy wife number three. It was a good thing that when Drew actually had the inclination to spend time in a hotel for the weekend, he had the good sense to do it in downtown Milwaukee where no one gave him a second look.

Maddy stopped in the hallway before she made it to his door. Her attention was taken by something on the bulletin board just outside. She seemed startled. And when she drew herself up and walked through the door, she stopped cold when she saw him. She looked harried as if her mind was racing in a million different directions at once.

"What's wrong?" Drew asked, ushering her into his office and then closing the door. Sam and his secretary could still see them, but they couldn't hear what Maddy had to say.

Maddy didn't answer but fumbled with her purse. Drew

asked again. This time slower. "Something is bothering, honey, what is it?"

The *honey* just slipped out. Drew regretted it immediately, especially using it in this setting.

Maddy didn't even seem to notice.

"What did you say?" she asked.

"Maddy, look at me."

She let her purse fall and looked at him.

"I left you less than ninety minutes ago. You were fine then. Now you're not. What happened?" Drew half sat on the edge of his desk, leaning over her slightly. He'd have held her arms, but he knew he had an audience.

Something in his tone or countenance must have cut through the fog in her brain because she was looking at him clearly now. She was hiding something from him. He was sure of it, but he knew her well enough to know she wasn't going to reveal her secrets until she was good and ready. No interrogation, no matter how hard or gentle, was going to change that. Madelyn Grace had been a stubborn child. There was no indication that trait had lessened over the years. "Tell me what's wrong."

Maddy swallowed hard. She pushed back in her chair. She fiddled with the bracelet she wore above her watch on her left wrist. Then she looked away from him, down and to the left, and lied to him. "Nothing's wrong, Drew," she said, looking back into his eyes. "I'm just worried about Ruby. She's got some kind of bug or something. Maybe not a bug, but something's just not right with her." Well, that last bit was true. But the first part wasn't.

It irked him that Maddy felt like she couldn't be honest

with him about what was going on in her life. Then it hit him. It wasn't Drew Selleck she couldn't be honest with, it was the Town of Gibraltar's police chief she couldn't or wouldn't talk to. Well, that revelation didn't make him feel any better. In fact, it made him suspicious, wary, and interested in digging into where Maddy had been and what she'd been doing—more so than the checks he'd already done.

She must have seen the suspicion in his eyes because she grew formal and reserved. "Why am I here, Drew?"

The way she said it, Drew guessed she already knew. Curious and curiouser. One thing Drew would stake his life on was that Maddy Grace was no thief.

Drew got up from the edge of his desk and moved around behind it. He stood high over Maddy with the large expanse of his desk between them. They were no longer on even ground. This was Drew's realm, and he ran it as such.

"There have been a number of break-ins at marinas up and down the coast. Boats in at least three towns have been burgled."

Maddy stiffened at the word *burgled* but said nothing.

"You've been spending time down at the marina in Fish Creek, and Dad mentioned you occasionally go up to Ephraim to paint at the marina there, as well."

Still nothing from Maddy but rigid silence.

"I was wondering if you've seen anything suspicious, or anyone hanging around who looks like they shouldn't be there."

Maddy sat up in her chair and leaned in. She didn't

answer his question, which was interesting in and of itself, but instead she countered with one of her own. "What was taken?"

Drew didn't see any harm in telling her. The news would be common knowledge in town shortly anyway. Besides, he hoped if he opened up to her, she'd feel comfortable enough to open up to him. "That's the weird thing. Some of the boats are missing some clothing and toiletries, but not all of their clothes. Some are missing canned goods and other food items. Cash and jewelry and electronics that could easily be sold have been left untouched."

Maddy sighed in what sounded like relief.

"There were also notes left on those boats next to cut flowers in tin cans, usually roses. Probably pilfered from local gardens. Earlier in the season tulips were left, as well."

"What did the notes say?"

Drew looked at her hard, judging every facial expression. "'Sorry.' The notes all said 'Sorry.'"

Maddy's lips moved upward in a micro smile. She looked down, regained her more serious composure, and asked, "What would happen to this person who took food and clothing if you caught them?"

"I'd arrest them and charge them with theft and criminal trespass. Whoever this is, they are stealing, Maddy."

Maddy shook her head no and said, "Right. I get that, Drew. Seems a little silly to me to prosecute someone who's hungry and sorry, but hey, that's your job. I get it."

Now he just felt like a vindictive ass. How did this

woman have the power to twist him up in knots?

"Maddy that is *exactly* my job, and I *will* do it."

Maddy just nodded.

"Maddy, that's not the extent of the break-ins. Some of the boats are missing the contents of their owner's safes. Jewelry, cash, firearms, art, are among the property taken from the other boats."

Maddy narrowed her eyes. "Were there notes and flowers left on those boats?"

"No."

Maddy stood. "Okay, then. I wish you luck catching your bad guy. Sorry I can't help you."

She was at the door and ready to open it when Drew said, "Maddy, if you know anything, anything at all, and you don't tell me now, that makes you an accomplice after the fact."

Maddy's back stiffened. She gripped the door handle so hard her knuckles turned white.

"That's a crime, Maddy."

"I'll see you in class, Drew. Have a good rest of your day." With that, Madelyn Grace sailed out of his office, never once looking back. She studiously avoided looking at his bulletin board on the way out.

Maddy was many things. Stubborn, loyal, fiercely independent, and secretive among them. What she wasn't was a thief or a liar. She hadn't told him the truth, but if he looked back at her word choice, she really hadn't lied either. And she was no good at hiding her feelings. He knew she really was worried about Ruby and her health. He knew she enjoyed spending time with him and wanted to spend more. He also knew she was protecting someone or something, and that she'd continue to do so as long as her own internal code of honor told her it was the right thing to do. Even if it landed her in jail.

The thought of Maddy behind bars for any period of time sickened him. If she wouldn't protect herself, he'd find a way to do it for her. With or without her compliance.

He left his office, stopped at Sam's desk, and gave Sam his notes. "Maddy hasn't seen anyone hanging 'round the marina who raised her suspicions. Guess we'll just have to solve this one the old- fashioned way. I'll stake out the marina here. You head up to Ephraim. Check out Sister Bay if there's nothing happening there. Tomorrow we'll check out Egg Harbor."

Sam jumped up, happy to get out of the office. "You got it boss."

Sam beat Drew out of the office, which was Drew's intent. He called to his secretary, "We're out, Sally. If you need me, use the radio. If Madelyn Grace calls, use my cell."

Sally gave him a smile and a wave.

Once Drew was in the hall where Sally couldn't see him from her desk, he went to the bulletin board, scrutinizing every piece of paper until he found it. "Ah, hell," he said out loud.

There, almost hidden behind a flyer announcing Jazz in the Park, was a grainy photo of a missing child. Judging from the date given in the notice, the girl would have turned eighteen by now, so few resources would be expended actually searching for her.

There was no mistaking that face. It was the face of the older girl in Maddy's painting—the one serving tea to a young version of his daughter.

"Oh, Maddy, what have you gotten yourself into?"

CHAPTER FOURTEEN

October 30
137lbs. No self-help mantras in 30 days.

Maddy had seen Rose Kelly periodically since the first day they met on the Mackenzie boat, but never again at the Fish Creek marina. After the first week of painting at the marina, Maddy feared she'd never see the girl again. Then she set up her easel and her chair at the small lakefront park at the end of a dead-end street just down from the White Gull Inn. She had to get there early, before the tourists filled the park.

That's when she saw Rose again. Clean and showered and wearing clothing that actually fit. From the fit of clothes there was no mistake Rose was pregnant. Very pregnant. Rose came up beside her and simply said, "Hello."

That was six weeks, and twelve lunches ago. In that time Rose and Maddy had become friends. Maddy always had a coffee cake, and a small bag of pre-made sandwiches, fruit, and vegetables with her. Most of the time when they were done talking, Rose took the bag of food. She always took the coffee cake. Unlike Maddy, Rose adored cherries.

They talked about their views on life, art, even politics. They spoke about very personal feelings, but by mutual agreement, never about how Rose came to be on the Mackenzie boat. Maddy didn't know what Rose was running from, or if indeed, she was running at all. Maddy had gotten Rose a part-time job at the Irish Shop in town. She was paid cash and allowed to stay in the small efficiency apartment above the shop. Maddy didn't think Rose was a criminal, but she was afraid Drew might not see it the same way, so she didn't tell him.

"What are you going to do when the baby comes?" Maddy asked Rose now as they sat eating their lunches at the picnic table outside the Irish shop.

"I'm going to give her up for adoption," Rose said, rubbing her extended belly.

Maddy smiled. "You know you're having a girl?"

"Just a feeling I have," Rose answered.

Maddy set her sandwich down. She didn't want to scare Rose away, especially not now, but she had to ask, "Have you gotten any pre-natal care? Do you have a doctor?"

Rose stiffened. "My baby is healthy, Maddy. I'd know if she weren't. You know I don't have any insurance. I don't have a home to go to although now that I'm not a minor anymore, they can't put me back in care. I can make my own home now."

"Of course, you can. I'll help," Maddy said.

"You've already helped, Maddy. You made me believe

I'm worth saving. I'll never doubt that again."

Maddy didn't know how to respond to that, so she just hugged Rose tight, not realizing that was the last time she'd see her for many years to come.

. . .

"Mom, you're late," Julie said as Maddy rushed through the door of the dance studio.

Julie was already in her tap shoes, anxious to begin. Maxie was still putting the last bit of their routine together, and it was making Maddy crazy. Julie hadn't wanted to tap with her when they started. Now, six weeks later, she was stretching and practicing twenty minutes early every time.

"I'm here. I'm exactly on time. I—"

"You won't be 'on time' by the time you get your shoes on."

Maddy cocked her head at her daughter. Things hadn't been as charged between her and Julie. They had been slowly building an adult mother-daughter relationship over the past six weeks. Still, they weren't on level ground yet. Things could turn rocky fast if Maddy said the wrong thing. Things could also get better if she said that right thing. Maddy took in Julie's unusual anxiety and decided to take a risk.

"Okay, my shoes are on," Maddy said standing. "Want to tell me what's bugging you?"

The sleigh bells on the door chimed and Julie's fiancé of nearly nine years walked through the door. He spotted Maddy, gave her a curt nod, then approached Julie.

Maddy eavesdropped unabashedly. She'd never liked Mathew Cane. That was a large cause of the rift between her and Julie. The fact that Maddy called Mathew a self-centered manipulative ass who only cares about improving his status may have been part of the problem, as well. In her defense, Mathew was manipulative, spiteful, and overly concerned with appearances. Maddy could have looked past most of that if she thought Mathew Cane actually loved her daughter. She didn't.

Mathew whispered in a voice meant to carry, "I thought you'd be done by now."

Julie touched his arm, then rubbed up and down, trying to physically soothe him. Then she answered him in that overly solicitous voice she only used around Mathew, the voice that grated on Maddy's nerves and made her wish she could smite Mathew Cane with fireballs from her eyes. "No, love, I told you dance *starts* at seven, not that it ends at seven. We haven't started yet."

Mathew turned petulant and whiny. "I don't know why you have to come to this when I'm here. I've got to go back to Germany soon, you know. I flew all this way just to see you."

Julie kept rubbing.

Maddy kept seething.

"I know and I appreciate it. Mom and I have the gala coming up, and we only have a few more practices to nail this routine. I'll make it up to you. I promise."

Maddy had heard quite enough. She stopped pretending to put her dance bag in order, and she headed toward the door. She didn't get away fast enough because she heard Mathew's nasty, "Fine. I'll come back in an hour."

Maddy got to the door just as Drew was coming in.

Mathew pushed past her with a mumbled, "Madelyn," and shouldered Drew as he left.

Drew startled at Mathew's rudeness, and asked Maddy, "Who was that?"

Maddy looked up, inordinately pleased to see him. The last month and a half had been slow torture laughing with him. Dancing so closely with him. Being held by him. Only to have him kiss her forehead when they said good-night. It was pleasant and sweet and driving her slowly insane. Maddy pulled him into the dance studio and into a corner away from Julie—who looked like someone just kicked her puppy.

When Maddy was sure they wouldn't be overheard, she told him, "That was my future son-in-law."

Drew looked back at the now empty entrance like he wanted to attack it.

Maddy almost kissed him.

"You're kidding?"

"No such luck, I'm afraid. I only wish it were a joke."

"What an ass. A very rude ass. The way he addressed you was like a slap in the face."

Maddy smiled at him. She appeared overly pleased with his response. "I'm used to it."

Drew didn't like that answer at all. "You should never have to get used to that. Doesn't Julie stop it?"

Maddy's eyes flashed to her daughter. She looked as sad as Drew had ever seen her. "No, not anymore. It's like she's brainwashed. Every time she tried to stick up for me, he got nastier. I think she just gave up. He's been in Germany for the last three months for work. He's only back now for a few days before he flies back for three more months."

Drew put his arm around Maddy's shoulders, an intimacy she'd allowed for over a month now. Arm around the shoulder. Holding hands in the park. Snuggling on the couch watching chick-flicks, and the occasional Bruce Willis, Sylvester Stallone, or Jason Statham movie. He'd dared all of it. What he hadn't dared to do was trust himself to take those intimacies any further. He loved her. He was pretty sure she loved him. But, she still hadn't told him about Julie yet, and until she did, he wasn't sure Maddy would ever trust him. Certainly not enough to marry him.

Drew led her to where Julie was stretching, waiting for Maxie to start their lesson. Drew wasted no time trying to right the wrong he'd just witnessed. "Was that your boyfriend just leaving?"

Julie looked at him and seemed to lose some of her anxiousness. They'd become friends over the last weeks. So much so, he stopped by her clinic several times a week just to say hi. Since Peter was generally around and invited into the conversation, it hadn't seemed odd to Julie at all. They even met for coffee every Wednesday morning before tap class so Drew could ask her questions about Maddy. Julie, for whatever reason, liked the idea of her mother dating, so she was happy to help. Along the way, Drew learned quite a lot about the woman his daughter had become. She wasn't quite the jaded millennial she pretended to be.

"My fiancé, Drew. You know I'm engaged."

"I would have liked to meet him, but he pushed passed your mother so quickly on the way out the door, that was impossible."

Julie flushed. "He's jealous of my time, that's all. He's got to leave in a few days, and he's frustrated I'm here and not at home with him."

Drew took that to mean the kid wasn't getting laid as much as he thought he should have so he was pouting and publicly punishing Julie for it. "Does that sound right to you?"

Whatever response Julie would have given was forestalled by Peter Blake running through the door. "Doc, you gotta come right now," Peter said heaving. He was having trouble catching his breath.

Drew recognized controlled panic when he saw it. He approached Peter calmly. "What is it Pete?"

"I've got a woman in exam room number two. I've called emergency services down in Sturgeon Bay but there was a four-car pile-up, and they're at least two hours out. She's bleeding, Drew, and the baby won't wait."

Julie turned to Maddy and said, "I'm going to need you and Drew to come with me. I don't have the staff for emergency deliveries. You're it, and we're on deck whether any of us is ready or not. Are you with me?"

Drew ushered them all into his Jeep, put the siren on, and drove the few blocks to Julie's clinic.

CHAPTER FIFTEEN

When they got to the clinic, Julie and Peter ran into the examining room, leaving Drew and Maddy in the lobby. Drew was immediately on the phone to Sturgeon Bay emergency services. Paramedics were indeed more than an hour out.

Drew put his hand over his cell phone and shouted back to Julie, "I need an update, kid. Got the paramedics on the line."

"She's crowning now, Drew. Unless they can be here in the next few minutes, they're not going to make it in time."

"How's the mother?" Drew asked, relaying the question from the paramedics now on speaker. "Strong. Healthy. No visible trauma."

"You got a name on the mother?"

No response but a low scream.

"Name's going to wait. Mom's a little busy right now," called out Julie.

"Do you need me to keep the paramedics on the line?"

"No, I'll call them when I need them."

Pause.

Another long grunting-scream.

"Time to let mama and me do our jobs, Chief," said Julie.

Drew ended the call and walked over to Maddy, took her in his arms and said, "Nothing to do now, honey, but wait."

They hadn't been together for Julie's birth, but they were together when this child's soft cry rent the air.

Maddy started to cry.

Drew held her in a long embrace while the tears flowed. Finally, he called out, "Julie, honey, I need to know how baby and mom are doing."

Peter walked out, holding the tiny, red-faced infant in his arms. The baby had pitch-black hair, lots of it. "Seven pounds, eleven ounces, twenty-one inches long of healthy all-American baby-girl," Peter said, grinning from ear to ear. "And I helped bring her into the world. How lucky am I?"

Peter sounded so pleased with himself and so sincerely grateful to be part of this child's entrance into the world, Maddy couldn't help but smile. She was feeling pretty blessed to be a small part of the miracle too. "May I hold her?" Maddy asked.

"Sure, you can," Peter said, handing Maddy the tightly-wrapped newborn. She wasn't crying now, and her tiny eyes were open, although she couldn't see clearly just yet. A tiny palm opened and Maddy put the tip of her pinky into it, watching as the small fingers did their best to wrap around it.

She looked up at Drew who was smiling at her with all the love in his heart shining in his eyes. "Julie only weighed five pounds, eight ounces when she was born. She was so tiny. This little girl seems even tinier than I remember Julie being. It's funny how you forget the exact details, but the feeling lives on in your heart."

Drew came up to Maddy and kissed her forehead. "I'm sure you were scared—and elated. I'm sorry I wasn't there then. I am here now." Drew smiled as Maddy's breath caught in her chest. It was the closest he'd come to intimating that he suspected he was Julie's father. He let the fact that he'd welcome her telling him wash over her as he asked, "Can I hold her?"

Julie chose that moment to walk out of her makeshift delivery room. She came over to check the baby, then picked her up and placed her in Drew's arms. Drew thought he heard some rustling around in the back, but then his world was filled with newborn baby, and something vital, elemental, and primal shifted inside him. Whatever happened in this girl's life, he wanted to be there to pave the way, to tear down walls, to make every moment go smoothly. It made no sense. But then loving one woman since they were both seven years old didn't make much rational sense either.

Julie smiled at him.

Drew would swear every day for the rest of his life the baby smiled at him.

He looked over at Maddy and she smiled at him.

Drew had no idea how long the three adults in the lobby let him get lost in a world where there was nothing but him and the baby. But when he came back to earth and reluctantly handed Julie the baby, he said, "I really need that name now, sweetheart. You and I have to finish the official business now. I've also got get mom and baby to a hospital."

Julie nodded. "Come on back. Mom was resting, but medically thriving when I left her. She should have no trouble answering all your questions."

Drew walked back to the examining room with Julie.

The examining table was empty, save for a note that had one word scrawled across the top. *Sorry.* There was a pen drawing of a rose under the script.

...

Two days later, a signed and legally executed affidavit arrived on Drew's desk. It had been executed weeks earlier according to the stamp and the date seal. It read in part:

By this affidavit I, the undersigned, acknowledge that I am the mother of baby "X," named by me, baby Kelly Rose, understanding I have no legal right to demand that my daughter or son carry that name once legally adopted, do hereby state my intent that Madelyn Grace of Fish Creek, Wisconsin, be the legal guardian of my child yet to be born alive. Should said child be born to me, it is my intent that baby Kelly Rose immediately, or as soon thereafter as is medically practicable, be put into Madelyn Grace's care and custody. It is my hope and my intent that baby Kelly Rose be formally adopted by Madelyn Grace.

There was some additional legalese that Drew read through until he got to the last line. He'd read many affidavits and not one had ended with a straight forward statement of fact that took his breath away. The last line read:

Madelyn Grace is the best person I know; I want her to raise and love my baby as she raised and loved her own. Any other result is unthinkable to me.

Signed,

Rose Kelly, aged 18 years. Enclosed is a sample of my DNA which I have also sent directly to Probate Court, to Chief Selleck of the Gibraltar Police Department, and to attorney Bill Haviland of Chicago who was recommended to me by Anne Gallager of The Rooster, Fish Creek. My lawyer also retains a sample of my DNA to prove I am baby X's mother. I hereby certify that I am not married at the time of this affidavit and that the father of my child is no longer living.

Drew called his secretary into his office. He had Sally make five copies of the affidavit and authenticated all five. He then put one of the duplicate originals in his office safe to ensure that HSD, Health and Human Services, didn't lose it. They wanted young adoptive parents. Not guardians who were in their forties.

Then he went straight to his daughter's clinic with his deputy and showed her the image he'd ripped from his bulletin board of the missing girl. He asked Julie if the woman who gave birth in her examining room was indeed the girl in the notice.

Julie's eyes had widened. "Yes. Definitely."

Drew left Sam to take a formal statement detailing everything Julie remembered. Then he went to The Rooster.

He found Bill Haviland sitting at the counter, drinking coffee as he contentedly watched the owner, Anne Gallager, walk by.

Only when he finished with Bill did he go to Zabler jewelers in Ephraim. He'd been smart during his career. He put aside and invested what he made in his short stint in the pros. He'd also been wise enough not to purchase the three-carat diamond his first wife ultimately got from her second husband. He saved that money instead. Then he invested when it made sense to do so. He'd also gotten very lucky.

Now he could buy the ring he'd wanted to give Maddy since he was single-digits old. Whether she chose to spend the rest of her life with him or not, the ring was hers. She was the mother of his child—a child that despite her deplorable choice in fiancé, was pretty wonderful.

Maddy was also, as Rose Kelly so eloquently stated, the best person Drew knew. She was his best friend, the only woman who could make him want to pull out his hair one minute and then sink into and loose his soul in the next. Maddy was his heart.

And he'd lose his shirt if he told the owner of Zabler jewelers that. So, Drew toned it down to 11. He walked out of Zabler's with a 2.40-carat, old European-cut diamond in a platinum art deco setting, surrounded with French-cut sapphires. The diamond's cut was fair and its color was low—somewhere in the M range on the GIA scale. It was far from perfect. And yet it was magnificent.

Exactly like Maddy.

Now all he had to do was convince her to have him for

the rest of her life.

The upshot? He was doing his best to bring her a baby for Christmas.

CHAPTER SIXTEEN

Maddy had baby Kelly with her for the first seventy-two hours. She didn't sleep much, which she expected. What she didn't expect, was Julie's help. Julie had all but moved in with her. *That* she didn't mind. Mathew, well, he was a different story.

"You know you don't have to get up every time she cries," Maddy said, as she cradled Kelly to her chest.

"I know, Mom. I want to be here."

"What about Mathew?"

"I'm taking Mathew to the airport in the morning."

"Isn't that early?"

"Yes," Julie said.

The look in Julie's eye made Maddy leave it alone. Julie would tell her in her own time about what was going on between her and Mathew. Or, she wouldn't. There wasn't much Maddy could do about it either way.

"They're coming to take Kelly away from me today," Maddy said.

"That's not going to happen, Mom. Drew isn't going to

let it."

Maddy smiled up at Julie from the couch. She was holding Kelly Rose, feeding her from a bottle she'd prepared the night before. Looking at Julie as she held this newborn, Maddy wondered where the time had gone. It seemed like only minutes since Julie was in her arms. "I'm not prepared for this, love. I mucked it up so badly the first time. That you turned out as well as you did is on you … And Ruby." Ruby had done so much for them both.

"Don't forget Jackie. Jackie Schneider did more than her fair share too," Julie said, taking a seat beside her. She lifted the now sleeping infant from Maddy's arms, setting the bottle aside, as she kissed the infant's brow. "You know, you're right Mom," Julie said, looking her mother in the eye. "You hardly did a thing. There's absolutely no reason for you to believe you could possible do nothing again."

Then Julie got up, took Kelly to the crib she'd helped Drew assemble and put the baby back to sleep. "Good night, Mom," she said, coming back to kiss Maddy on the top of the head. "Try to get some sleep. There will be plenty of nothing to do again in the morning."

Maddy said nothing.

And just like that she knew she her daughter was back.

She also knew she had a whole new adventure in front of her. One worth fighting for. The first thing she was going to do when daylight broke was ask Drew Selleck to marry her. Sure, he'd balk for a while. Then she'd offer to dance with him every day for the rest of his life. She thought that might just do the trick.

First, she had to tell him and Julie about one another.

Maddy wasn't looking forward to the fallout from that, but it was well past time.

...

Judge Vincent Mayweather sat in his chambers, wondering why he needed to hear a guardianship case on a Wisconsin safe haven baby when he'd rather be making pumpkin pie with his wife for Thanksgiving dinner. He'd grant the guardianship. He had to. What he didn't have to do was allow the subsequent adoption.

The woman was too old. Who wanted to adopt a baby at forty-four anyway?

She wasn't married. Not that she had to be. Plenty of single women adopted babies in their forties. Most of them had real jobs, that was for certain. But this one had enough income. She also had a stable home, even if she'd only been there since July. She'd grown up in the Door, so odds were, she had people there, even if she didn't realize their value.

Yes, Judge Vincent Mayweather had every intention of granting Madelyn Grace's petition for guardianship of the baby named Kelly Rose. He'd planned on ordering the adoption as well, as soon as Ms. Grace met the Wisconsin state residence requirement of six months. But as he sat in chambers, *not* making pumpkin pie with his wife, he decided he wasn't going to tell her that. He'd play devil's advocate first. He did, after all, have a duty to make certain this baby had a good home.

He looked sternly at Madelyn Grace who cradled the

sleeping baby in her arms. No easy feat for a grandfather who enjoyed the company of children far more than he'd ever admit. "So, tell me, Ms. Grace, exactly why I should believe you'd be a good mother to this child."

Before Madelyn could answer, her daughter, Julie Grace, shot up out of her chair. "I'll tell you why," she said.

"No, you won't," Judge Mayweather answered.

"But—"

"No buts, young lady. Not until my court reporter is here at any rate." Judge Mayweather pressed a button on his desk and said, "Judy, would you come in here please? And bring extra paper for your machine." He looked up at Julie Grace, still standing and more than ready to be heard. "I've got a doctor here who's bound and determined to be heard on the merits of being raised by a single mother."

For the next twenty minutes Julie Grace pontificated about exactly that. When she was done and the guardianship had been granted, both Maddy and Drew were at a loss about what to say.

Mathew Cane wasn't. He ended the engagement and went back to Germany where it turned out he'd gotten another woman pregnant. That woman just happened to be the daughter of a German parliamentarian. A step up for him from the daughter of what he called a second-rate artist who was never going to somebody.

Well, he was wrong about that. Maddy Grace had just heard her daughter say she was a good mother. On the record. There was a transcript and everything. She also was assured by Judge Mayweather that Kelly Rose would be her daughter in the eyes of the law by January 15th—six months to the day of when Maddy could prove she officially moved to Fish Creek. The letter of law had to be abided by, the judge had said. And so it was.

All that remained to be seen was whether or not Kelly Rose Grace would be adding the name Selleck to her court documents.

CHAPTER SEVENTEEN

Julie arrived early to her second to last dance class before the Thanksgiving Gala. All the tiny-tots who were doing a ballet number to music from *Beauty and the Beast* were busy dancing away. As their program came to an end, and MaryEllen walked them to their parents, Julie heard MaryEllen talking about her mother.

"It's just odd, that's all, and not at all natural, to be adopting a baby at her age," MaryEllen said to a young mother as she scooped up her little cherub and shucked her into a miniature-sized parka. Before the woman could say anything in response, a father piped in.

He took his daughter by the hand and said to MaryEllen. "Great class, MaryEllen. We're looking forward to the gala." Then he paused and continued with a puzzled look on his face, "You know my older sister has been trying to have a child for years. She and my brother-in-law tried every fertility option they could afford. Nothing. No luck whatsoever. I can't think of a person better suited for motherhood than my sister. She's funny, caring, and she's a great aunt."

MaryEllen interjected, "Susie sure is. She's the greatest!"

The little girl holding her father's hand who couldn't have been more than three or four interjected, "Aunt Susie is the greatest!"

Her father picked her up and kissed her cheek. Smiling down as his daughter, he said, "She sure is, sweetheart." Then he looked at MaryEllen. He lost his smile. "She's also forty-seven years old." Then he nodded politely, turned and walked away.

Julie doubted MaryEllen got the man's point. But that didn't matter. She did.

. . .

The night of the gala came, and Maddy was a nervous wreck. She'd learned every step of her tap dance with Julie. She loved the choreography and the Bruno Mars song. It was challenging for her, and she felt every muscle in her body, something she was pretty certain Julie didn't feel. Julie was far more talented and quick to learn the moves. She also had natural rhythm which Maddy had long since determined was *not* a teachable skill—mostly because she hadn't picked it up yet.

None of that mattered. What mattered was she was dancing. And she was loving it. She hadn't kept up on her daily meditations, but she did say a prayer of thanks every morning for her family, her health, her art, her little General—even when he woke her up barking before dawn at the squirrels infiltrating her bird feeder. She was also thankful for Drew although what she was going to do to get that man to actually sleep with her again, she didn't know. She prayed for that as well, but so far, she hadn't heard the Almighty whispering in her ear.

Maddy sighed, looking in her bathroom mirror. She put the finishing touches on the over-the-top make-up Maxie insisted all her dancers wear. Who the heck thought quarter-inch false eyelashes were a good idea? "I swear," Maddy grumbled to her reflection, "if I have to be held by that man as he wiggles his hips into me one more time without tearing off his clothes in front of God and everybody, then I ought to be a candidate for sainthood."

Julie popped her head into the bathroom. "Never going to happen, Mom. Sainthood is for actual saints."

"Thanks a lot."

"Your welcome. Now fix your lipstick and let's go. *That* man is waiting downstairs to take us to the ball."

"It's a gala," Maddy said under her breath.

"I know it's a gala, Mom. Hurry up."

Maddy added another layer of Gypsy Red lipstick to her already scarlet-red lips and went downstairs to greet *that* man. General was sitting in his lap when she arrived. Kelly Rose was safely ensconced in J.T.'s arms—*not* crying or spitting up. Julie was tapping her foot in nervous exasperation, telegraphing to all who were paying attention that she wanted to leave five minutes ago and her mother was making them late. And Ruby was smiling at her, looking radiant, if a bit too thin, in her deep-purple beaded gown.

Maddy stopped at the bottom of the stairs to take it all in.

She'd moved back home in July. Now she was surrounded with people, and a dog, she loved. She'd also lost twenty-three pounds without doing her daily meditations. Someone, somewhere was looking out for her. A fact for which Madelyn Grace was profoundly grateful.

CHAPTER EIGHTEEN

"Stop fidgeting," Drew said to Maddy. She'd already finished her dance with Julie, and she'd rocked it. He couldn't imagine why she was nervous about their dance. They'd practiced it long and hard enough. He couldn't wait for it to be over. Holding her while she swayed into him with that take-me-now look on her face was killing him. He didn't know how much longer he had it in him to play gentleman to Maddy's lady.

The effort was making him grumpy.

"I am not fidgeting. I'm stretching."

"Then try not to rub me while you're doing it," he snapped.

"I am not rubbing you," Maddy snapped back, pushing out the stage curtain as she gestured a bit more violently than she should have. When the curtain moved she got an upfront view of the white linen-clad tables surrounding the stage.

Then came her daughter's voice over the microphone. Maddy had forgotten that Julie was going to announce her dance with Drew. "Great," she said grumbling at Drew. "Now everyone saw us bickering before the show."

"We can hear you too, Mom," Julie announced with a smile.

Maddy's face flamed as she shot Drew a narrow-eyed look, wondering as she did it, why she was so irritated with him.

"And those two arguing behind the curtain are our next performers," Julie said.

Drew gripped Maddy's hand more tightly than he needed to. He looked straight ahead at the curtain. A definite tick hammered at his clenched jaw. Evidently, he was as irritated with her as she was with him.

"Ladies and gentlemen," Julie continued, an obvious smile in her voice, "may I introduce my parents, Madelyn Grace and Drew Selleck. If they don't kill each other first, they'll be performing the rumba to *Bolero*."

Drew pulled her out onto the stage just as the shock of Julie's words hit her.

She stumbled over one of the sound cords. Drew held her firm, keeping her on her feet. He led her to center stage without a word. Then he smiled down at her as the spotlight illuminated their starting position—their *frame* as Maxie called it. "Cat's out of the bag now, darlin'. I guess you'll have to marry me."

Everyone at the front tables heard him, including Julie who still held the microphone just off stage.

Then she lifted that microphone, winked at Drew, and said to the entire crowd—which was most of Fish Creek, Egg Harbor, and Ephraim, "In case those of you in the cheap seats missed it, my mom's finally marrying my dad."

After a few catcalls and risqué comments, Drew whispered in her ear, "Dance with me, woman. Now, and every day for the rest of my life."

Maddy did just that.

Most of those dances were performed naked.

With huge smiles on both of their faces.

EPILOGUE

Maddy and Drew found out about Ruby's diagnosis before Christmas. Ruby and J.T. told them with Julie at their side to answer their medical questions. Julie did just that with a straight-forward thoroughness that had Maddy feeling even more proud of the woman their daughter had become.

J.T. and Ruby were unapologetic for telling Julie that Drew was her father. Drew was flabbergasted that the reason Julie spent all those lunches with him was because she wanted to get to know her father without him having to feel like he needed to play dad. A role he now talked about to anyone who'd listen.

Maddy and Drew were married with their family and General by their side. The General wore a bow-tie as did Peter who performed the ceremony, having become an online ordained minister. In addition to being Julie's assistant, and the yoga and ballroom dance teacher, he had also attended seminary for three years. At the time of Maddy and Drew's wedding, Peter was also completing his doctoral thesis in the real-life romantic effects of reading Jane Austin on millennials. He was also actively pursuing Julie who had yet to give in.

Kelly Rose Grace Selleck would go on to join her sister practicing naturopathic medicine, specializing in pediatrics and pain management in cancer patients. She would have two daughters of her own and adopt the baby boy of one her patients. All would grow healthy and strong. Two would serve in the military. One would become a college professor at the encouragement of Uncle Peter.

Kelly Rose received a dozen roses every October 30th, her birthday. There was no card attached, but Maddy would tell her stories about her biological mother's bravery every time the roses came. On the day she married, Kelly Rose met Rose Kelly. On the day of Maddy's funeral, exactly two months to the day after Drew's, Kelly Rose met Rose Kelly's two daughters. From that day on Kelly had three sisters and one perfect brother-in-law who helped deliver her and who, at least she thought, could do anything.

Ruby Grace Hodgkins died in J.T. Selleck's arms just shy of Kelly's fifth birthday. Even though Kelly hadn't yet started kindergarten when Ruby passed, she still had memories of Ruby. Most of which included cherry coffee cake and warm hugs.

When Kelly's daughters and son laid her to rest on Christmas day, eighty-seven years after her birth, they found an old photograph yellowed with age in the end table next to her bed. In the photo, baby Kelly Rose was held in J.T.'s arms. Ruby was dressed in a purple beaded gown, standing beside J.T. Drew Selleck, their grandfather, had one arm holding a funny looking white dog who seemed to be smiling. His other arm was wrapped around Maddy Grace. Julie Grace, who didn't take the name Selleck or Blake after she married, stood beside a grinning Peter who couldn't help but capture what was known then as a selfie stick in the photo.

The photo was inside a Christmas card, well-worn from having been read often over the decades. The message inside the Christmas card read:

My Christmas came in July when you came home.

By December you gave me yourself and not one, but two, babies to call my own.

Happy Christmas, Love.

I'll dance with you every day for the rest of my life.

Drew

Kelly Rose's grandchildren cried when they read the card. Every one of them. Because their grandparents had danced every day of their lives together.

So had their mother. Even when she danced by herself in the kitchen. Or, more often than not, barefoot with them.

And they danced, too, with their children.

Merry Christmas!

If you enjoyed, CHRISTMAS IN JULY, please leave a review on Amazon, Barnes and Noble, or Good Reads. Thank you. May every Blessing find you this Christmas and always. And if you get the chance, I hope you dance!

Leigh Morgan

AUTHOR'S NOTES

Wisconsin's Safe Haven Law is real and codified in Wis. Stats. Sec. 48.195. Under this law an infant up to three-days-old can be left with any employee of any: hospital, fire station, sheriff's office, police station, emergency medical services provider, or any other law enforcement agency in Wisconsin

Thank you Wisconsin – Thanks to you no infant need ever be abandoned again.

Leigh

In Plain Sight

Dedication

For Ewa – A woman of passion, strength and an inherent sweetness that radiates into whomever she meets.

Summer O'Hara is almost as wonderful as you.

Prologue

2002, the Museon Museum of Science in the Netherlands is burgled while housing an exhibit showcasing several royal jewels valued over 7.4 million pounds. No alarms sounded during or after the theft. Shattered glass housing the jewels was the only damage done to the museum (not counting the theft). Local and international newspapers used the word "baffled" to describe the mindset and progress of the local authorities searching for jewel thief or thieves.

2003, over 62 million pounds (British pounds sterling) in diamonds is stolen from the Antwerp Diamond Center in Belgium. The Antwerp Diamond Center holds 160 underground vaults used to house diamonds. Of the 160 vaults, 123 were emptied. Although one man with mafia connections was arrested and convicted (based on circumstantial evidence) for the crime, the diamonds were never recovered.

2005, 73 million British pounds sterling of diamonds is stolen from a cargo truck on its way to the Schiphol Airport.

2008, the Damiani showroom in Milan is broken into by slowly drilling a hole into the shop basement from a basement next door that was under construction. Thieves entered during a private showing dressed as security. They walked away with over 12.4 million pounds sterling of gold and jewels.

2008, the Harry Winston store in Paris is robbed. This robbery, of over 68 million pounds sterling worth of jewelry, made headlines not just for the sheer volume of jewelry stolen, but because the men who robbed the store did so dressed as women. No arrests have been made.

...

Jack Smith—not the name given at his birth, nor the name he used for any of his previous incarnations which were many—retired from active jewel procurement a decade ago. By any measure, he was an unmitigated success. He'd never been detained. He'd never been questioned. And, most importantly, he'd never been suspected in any of the robberies or burglaries he'd committed.

No one suspected him. No one butted into his business. No one questioned who or what he pretended to be.

Jack's criminality had been ridiculously easy. Not the theft part. That had been hard. It required planning for every contingency while maintaining the flexibility to improvise. It took every skill in his metaphorical toolbox to pull off each and every job.

Every job—until the last one. That one he enjoyed. Dressing as a woman to commit robbery had its own appeal, but it was holding the terrified and trembling employees at gunpoint that stirred his soul in a way Jack hadn't thought possible.

He didn't want to kill anyone. Not really. But making someone tremble with the need for self-preservation was a uniquely heady experience. One, that had he let it, would become addictive. That kind of power filled him with heat.

Provocative. Arousing. It gave him the kind of high that bordered on invincibility.

That's why he quit the acquisitions end of the business. Aside from the fact that he'd acquired far more than he could spend in a lifetime, no one was invincible. No high was worth the inevitable loss of control it bred. Acquisitions was a young man's game, and he hadn't been young a decade ago when he'd done his last hands-on acquiring.

Acquiring was hard. Selling, or rather underselling, by contrast, was proving ridiculously easy.

Jack had spent years alternating between shops in Chicago and Door County selling his "replica" line of jewelry without so much as a whisper or a raised eyebrow. No one questioned who he was or the authenticity—strictly speaking, a lack-thereof—of his product.

No one questioned.

Until Summer O'Hara came back to town.

Summer O'Hara had seen something she wasn't supposed to see. She waltzed right into his Ephraim store one morning while he and his assistant were still doing setup. It was the first big tourist weekend, Memorial Day weekend, and he was still unloading from his Chicago shop.

He had one of the Harry Winston rings out, a small one by Chicago standards, but big enough to capture the notice of the Ephraim prodigal flower child who fashioned herself a jewelry expert. He'd meant the ring to stay packed until his client came to pick it up, but his assistant placed it in with the vintage rings for sale.

Amateurs—the bane of those in the know. That held true for both Summer O'Hara and his assistant who was still so eager to please.

Summer O'Hara asked to see the ring. She noticed the distinctive Harry Winston hallmark, and her pulse picked up a beat. She wasn't good at hiding her excitement, but then normal people didn't hide their excitement the way thieves and organized criminals learned, by necessity, to hide theirs.

Jack had to tell her that the ring (a three carat, D color, Internally Flawless, brilliant cut center flanked by two tapered baguettes totaling .30 carats) had already been sold to a customer who was due to pick it up that very day. It was just bad luck that his "customer" arrived in time to meet Summer.

Summer O'Hara got a good look, not only at Jack's client but her car—complete with Illinois plates. His client's car was parked in Jack's small car park in front of his small house-like shop. No way Summer could have missed it. It was the only car in the lot besides Jack's decade-old Porsche Boxer and Summer's late model sub-SUV.

Summer stayed in his shop, eavesdropping through the

entire exchange while pretending to window shop as the cases were being set up. Once she looked at every partially completed case, Summer left. But not before taking another long glance at Jack's client.

That was strike one.

Strike two came three weeks later, the third week in June, when Summer again came into the shop when it opened, this time with one of her adult sons. Just like last time, Summer honed in on the case that housed the only stolen items in the store. His "replica" case.

The "replicas" included three original coins from the Atocha, each mounted as pendants in 24k yellow gold; an Art Deco Asscher cut 9.34-carat diamond engagement ring set in platinum with tapered bullet-cut diamonds totaling .40 carats that had been part of his safety deposit find; and a broach he'd made after taking the 60-carat vivid pink diamond, previously known as the "Flower of Scotland," from the tiara a Japanese billionaire had made for one of his daughters. Another of his safety deposit box finds from Antwerp's Diamond Center, the tiara housed colored diamonds of impeccable quality, ranging from 14 to 19 carats. His favorites included vivid yellow diamonds, more pink diamonds, a small blue diamond, and three green diamonds that appeared to change color due to their florescence.

The Asscher ring was from 1925. Jack knew that because he'd gotten rid of the dated inscription and the initials that accompanied it. He'd also eradicated the GIA certification number—no easy feat but one he had the expertise and the access to accomplish.

The 60-carat pink diamond Jack got as part of the same Antwerp job. He'd gotten far more than expected from that job, including the Atocha coins.

Jack took the Zoe Tiara apart, setting the center piece pink in a sterling silver broach. It galled him to put such a collector's gem—a gem that rivaled any collected by Graff or Winston—into anything but platinum, but he did it. The best place to hide something of potentially limitless value was to put it in plain sight. His clients loved that. It made them feel like they were flaunting theft and getting away with it.

The Art Deco diamond ring he placed in his *Immaculate Imposters* case. Most people wouldn't have raised a brow at the ring if they had reason to believe it wasn't real—it was rather gaudy in his opinion. Lovely in the way perfectly cut step cut diamonds are lovely, but gaudy. He'd seen many created diamonds, cubic zirconia and other diamond substitutes, made into rings this size. Not his preference, but then he'd rather steal diamonds than wear them.

The pink, the former Flower of Scotland, simply didn't look real. That was the beauty of what he'd accomplished. Jack Smith, jeweler extraordinaire, had made the real and exceptionally rare appear fake.

Genius.

And it had worked flawlessly for over a decade.

Until the morning Summer O'Hara walked into his store and zeroed in on the pink.

Her hand went to her chest as she inhaled deeply. Honestly, Jack thought he saw tears in her eyes as she asked to see it. It was the one piece in the case that didn't have a tag indicating that it was a "replica" of whatever it actually was. It was the one piece that looked like cut glass. Ostentatious set on its own, but the light hitting it refracted brilliantly, shooting out mesmerizing rainbows of color.

"Oh, Gus, look," Summer said to her son, who appeared bored but feigned interest because it seemed important to his mother. Summer pointed toward the broach. "It looks exactly like the Flower of Scotland in the Zoe Tiara."

To Jack's knowledge, the Zoe Tiara had appeared in trade magazines and in British Vogue only once. It wasn't well known. No princess had been photographed wearing it. There wasn't even a photo of Zoe wearing it. She'd been only seven years old when it was commissioned, and Jack had stolen it shortly after. It had never come up for auction, so there wasn't great opportunity for gem collectors to see it or for those who wrote about rare gems and jewelry to report on it.

Summer looked up at Jack as he stood behind the case, fingers curling into fists at his side, thankful the case hid his rising anger. He never expected anyone would recognize the Flower of Scotland. He certainly believed no one entering his Ephraim shop would have ever heard of the Zoe Tiara.

But then, Summer O'Hara wasn't ordinary. She was a flake. Today, Summer was dressed in a tie-dyed peasant blouse, jeans, and sandals that looked like they cost fifteen dollars at the local Wal-Mart. She had a high-quality emerald cut diamond she wore on her right hand. It looked like a replica of Grace Kelly's engagement ring, only much smaller.

If he didn't miss his guess—and he didn't—Jack estimated that the ring was worth about $35,000. Why a woman with the wherewithal to wear a ring like that didn't wear better shoes was anyone's guess.

And that attempt to pigeonhole Summer O'Hara into a box that clearly didn't fit was Jack's mistake. A mistake he'd already made once and was about to make again.

Summer gestured toward the broach expansively. She was definitely interested and just knowledgeable enough to be dangerous. "Can I please see that broach, Mr. Smith?"

Deflection. Jack tried that first. He'd learned long ago that the key to offending someone enough to make them leave was the kind of polite effusiveness that walked the razor's edge of being insulting but not insulting enough to get punched in the face.

Jack ignored Summer's request to see the pink and grabbed her waving right hand instead, giving her his best smarmy smile. "This is a lovely ring, Mrs. O'Hara. If you're interested in selling it like the other pieces of jewelry from your late husband, I'll give you eighteen thousand for it."

Summer went pale halfway through his question.

Summer's son turned mean before that.

Jack hadn't expected the violence of Summer's son's intervention. Gus Murphy grabbed Jack by the wrist and squeezed so hard Jack had no option but to release Summer's right hand. Jack, a man of quick reflexes and even quicker response to aggression, hadn't even seen it coming. One second, Gus was standing stock still. The next, he'd manacled Jack's wrist.

"You, and everyone else in this county, know my mother sold everything Geoffrey gave her to keep our family business afloat after Geoff's death. He wasn't the only one to lose everything in '08, but he managed to lose more than most." Gus gave one sharp nod toward his mother. "That ring is all my mother has left of Geoff. I'd sell the gallery before I'd let her sell that ring."

Gus still had ahold of Jack's wrist. His grip got tighter as his voice got lower and infinitely more threatening. "That ring is worth twice what you just offered and you know it." Gus's blue eyes shifted from angry to lethal. "Don't touch my mother again without her consent."

Just as Jack thought the bones of his wrist might snap, Gus Murphy released him. Gus stepped back, and when he spoke again the ice had left his eyes, and his tone was politely neutral. "Now, please show my mother that broach."

Jack's miscalculation of Summer's knowledge and her children's determination to protect her was Summer's strike three.

Jack was sorry for that.

Not because Summer O'Hara would have to die, but because her death would mean increased interest in the small Door County town of Ephraim, which meant increased traffic in his shop. Just the kind of attention that could complicate the constant funnel of funds he'd grown to rely on from the sale of his "replicas."

Without a word, Jack retrieved the broach from the locked case and handed it to a now subdued Summer O'Hara. Summer's enthusiasm for the piece had been deflated by his offer to buy her ring. She wasn't comfortable with her son's leashed aggression either. That was obvious by the way she looked down and away when Gus grabbed him.

Summer examined the broach critically for half a minute then turned the broach over in her hand, assessing everything over again from the back.

Gus noted the stamp Jack had used in the metal. "It's sterling, Mom. No one would set a pink diamond in sterling. Not even a small one."

Summer said nothing.

She reached into her purse with her free hand and pulled out a small 10x loupe. She held it to her eye, then brought the broach to it like a pro.

Jack had underestimated Summer O'Hara. And her son's devotion to her.

Summer lowered the broach away from her eye, put the loupe away, studiously avoiding Jack's gaze as she held out her hand, palm up with the broach cradled in it for him to take.

Before Jack could take it, his client walked through his front door, walking directly to Summer O'Hara. The woman took off her sunglasses, threw Gus, then Summer, a blinding smile that warmed her eyes and lit her face with the ethereal beauty only those blessed with good genes and supreme confidence could pull off. It was an *I'll-always-be-richer-than-you* smile. Every one of Jack's clients kept that smile in their arsenal.

His client held out her gloved hand to Summer. "I believe that," she said, nodding toward the broach nestled in Summer's outstretched palm, "belongs to me."

Summer O'Hara handed the broach to the woman. She'd seen the woman in Jack's store before, last time picking up a Harry Winston original. The woman was all long legs and straight long blond hair that looked like a wig, with an affecting smile that rose the hair on the back of Summer's neck. Summer had a knack for spotting people who were not who they pretended to be. Dangerous people.

She'd ignored the feeling with Jack Smith. She'd chalked it up to the affected superiority those living and working on Michigan Avenue in Chicago embodied. Oddly enough, it wasn't usually displayed by those working at Tiffany's or Georg Jensen or even Graff's in Chicago. Yet Jack had it.

Summer wasn't ignoring the warning signs any longer.

As soon as the broach left her hand, Summer grabbed Gus's hand and left Jack Smith's store. She'd never visited his sister store in Chicago. Now she never would.

"Thank you for your time, Mr. Smith." Summer pulled her twenty-nine-year-old son, who was a foot taller and nearly eighty pounds heavier than her, over the threshold and down the stairs toward the lot where she'd left her car.

Summer was in a hurry.

Certainty burned through her like boiling magma breaking the earth's crust. There was no time for half measures. As Hamlet would say, "Something is rotten in the state of Denmark." Ephraim, for all its Scandinavian roots, wasn't Denmark. Still, something *was* rotten in Ephraim and Jack Smith reeked of it.

"Why the rush, Mom?" Gus asked, extracting his hand

from his mother's. For a small woman, Summer O'Hara had one heck of a grip when she was on a mission. Which, more times than not, had something to do with her children. This time was different. Whatever was bothering Summer, it had to do with Jake Smith's shop. Gus shook his head. His mother had let her overactive imagination run amok with her crazy theory that Jack Smith was fencing jewels stolen by international jewel thieves. Gus didn't like the man, would have preferred to punch him in the face for trying to play his mother, but that didn't mean he was buying into his mother's fantasies.

Summer O'Hara needed a hobby. Gus would talk to his brother about having her take a more active role at the gallery. Maybe they could start selling a line of affordable jewelry. That might take her mind off Jack Smith. It may also take her mind off all the beautiful jewelry she'd been forced to sell after her second husband's death.

Summer stopped outside the door of her car. "Sorry, darling, I didn't mean to pull you out of the shop."

She had meant to do exactly that, but Gus didn't call her on it; he simply raised a brow and waited for her to finish.

"I'll have to skip lunch today." She looked at her watch. She'd replaced the Cartier that Geoff had given her for her fortieth birthday with a Citizen Eco-Drive which she claim to love just as much. Now for the first time, Gus felt the heat of helplessness flare. Someday he planned to get back every damned piece she'd been forced to sell, but for now, he had all he could do keeping the orchard, winery, gallery, and the house payments in check.

"Mom, don't do anything radical. Please."

His mother smiled. "Aside from the belly-dancing classes and the watercolor tattoo, when have you ever known me to do anything radical?"

Gus had a list. Instead of detailing it, he kissed his mother's head and said, "Drop me off at the winery then?"

"Of course," Summer said.

Her phone call could wait the thirty minutes it would take to get back home.

Little did Summer O'Hara know that the phone call she was about to make would be her last in this lifetime.

CHAPTER ONE

"Max, that crazy Irish lady from Door County is on line one for you," Jason, Max Scott's onetime partner and friend, shouted from across the room. "Main routed the call to me, but she's all yours, buddy. You made the mistake of calling her back the first time. Now you keep her."

Max waved Jason off with a shooing gesture that said, *yeah, I got it, you think I'm crazy too, now go away.*

Jason lifted his chin in acknowledgement, then went back to his desk.

Max wasn't sure if the call was good news or bad news. The first call he'd gotten from Summer O'Hara concerned a moderate to large Harry Winston diamond. There were plenty of legitimately purchased three to four carat diamonds available in shops that sold vintage jewelry, including e-Bay.

Max Scott had known his fair share of crackpot tipsters. Those who managed to be credible or crazy enough to make it past the tip-line screening, claiming some sort of information on high-value jewelry thefts, usually landed on his desk.

He should have learned his lesson about following questionable leads when he got transferred from the Miami field office back to Chicago. Miami didn't do questionable, which he'd done one too many times. That was how he found himself back in Chicago, where June hadn't figured out it was supposed to be warm.

Max was part of the FBI's Jewelry and Gem Theft Team of investigators stationed in various cities across the nation. In his career, he'd worked with Interpol to investigate and ultimately arrest a ring of thieves who committed heists from Milan to London to Miami. International criminals traveled from country to country, generally covering their tracks. That was part of the allure and a big part of the problem in trying to identify, and ultimately, apprehend them. That was the high point.

The low point was where he found himself now— fielding calls on local thefts, waiting for the phone to ring with that big case that would get him back into the game.

He'd been kicked out of Miami for chasing leads on a closed case from Antwerp. They arrested and ultimately convicted one man in Belgium for the 2003 Antwerp job, but the diamonds were never recovered. Max knew they were out there somewhere. He suspected at least one member of the ring was still active. He suspected that same member was involved in the Harry Winston theft in Paris, in which twenty percent of the haul was never recovered, and in the 2009 theft of over 40 pounds sterling worth of diamonds and jewelry from the Graff store in central London.

He'd chased every real lead that came his way.

None of them turned into anything solid.

Then he chased every iffy lead that came in. Some of which he thought were purposely planted to watch him spin his wheels. Frustrating, since he'd been chasing those leads since he inherited the case six years ago.

Again, his leads led to nothing.

His superiors hated the wasted time. More than that, they liked closed cases and hated that he continued to chase phantom leads that led nowhere, making the field office look bad. That's when he got shipped out of Miami and back to Chicago. Even Interpol didn't want to hear from him any longer.

He'd been assigned to an investigation on an organized theft ring out of Columbia that did business across Western Europe and a good portion of North America when the first call from Door County came in. He'd listened to Summer O'Hara. He'd been polite. He even took down the name of the shop and the proprietor and ran checks on both. No hits. Not even a civil complaint.

Still, something nagged him about Summer O'Hara's certainty. He couldn't define it, but it wouldn't go away. So he started a file. And he filed it away, doing nothing more on it. Following his personal promise *not* to go down the rabbit hole again. Worried they'd send him to Alaska next time.

Knowing he shouldn't, Max pushed the button next to the blinking light and put the receiver to his ear. "Max Scott," he said, more curtly than he should have.

A familiar, not-so-crazy voice said, "Agent Scott, I've

found the lost Flower of Scotland."

Max said nothing.

He couldn't formulate a response before his heart stopped beating and his breath caught painfully in his chest. The fact that the Zoe Tiara, which contained the Flower of Scotland as its centerpiece, had been part of jewelry stolen in Antwerp was never made public. Only those agents assigned to the investigation, the owners of items stolen, and those who had access to the Jewelers' Security Alliance database of stolen jewels, knew the Zoe Tiara had been stolen. Damn few people knew it existed. The only other group who could have known about the theft was the people who stole it.

Max swallowed hard and asked, "Is this Summer O'Hara?"

"Yes."

"Are you calling from your home?" Max asked, knowing she was. Her number and address came up on his screen. He also knew this call was being recorded, which he didn't need or want. He needed to get to Summer O'Hara and interview her in person.

"Yes."

"Stay where you are," Max said. He looked at his watch. "I'll be there in six hours. We'll talk then."

Max didn't wait for Summer O'Hara to confirm she understood. He wanted no more details recorded that could send him from Chicago to some place even colder. He disconnected the call.

Then he got up, walked to Jason's desk and said, "If she calls back, tell her I'll get back to her after the weekend. I'm heading out."

Jason looked at his watch. "It's barely noon."

"It's *after* noon on a beautiful Friday. I've already logged fifty hours this week. That's twelve more than you, partner." Max smiled what he hoped was an appropriately lascivious smile. He was out of practice on that score. It had a long time since he'd had cause to feel anything approaching lasciviousness.

"I've got a date," he lied.

A date long past due and a long drive to catch my white whale.

What Max didn't count on was that his whale attacked preemptively.

. . .

Max pulled into Ephraim later than he expected. Road construction and state troopers up and down I-94 had seen to that. It was 7:06 when he pulled into Summer O'Hara's driveway. Almost an hour later than he'd told Summer he'd be.

The first thing Max noticed as he approached the two-story Victorian-style house was how welcoming it appeared. There were bright flowers lining the sidewalk and around the home. Hanging flower baskets on the covered front porch appeared to wrap around the entire home. Windows stood open on the second floor, letting in the breeze off the lake that cooled the warm evening air.

As he walked up the curved concrete sidewalk, the idyllic image changed. Max couldn't define what worried him, but he sensed something was very wrong. That sense of dread magnified with every step he took, propelling him forward as he quickly scanned the yard and surrounding area. The house and adjoining backyard nestled into a tree dense hill that shot up at a steep angle, ending at the road about a hundred or so feet above. Max scanned the hill. Anyone could have been there watching him, but he couldn't make out movement in the trees.

Max stepped up onto the porch, noticing the camera high in the corner shooting video of him as he approached Summer O'Hara's door. Many people he knew had a doorbell app that took video and sometimes stills of anyone ringing their doorbell and notified their cell phone in real time with the video.

Hopefully, Summer O'Hara knew he was here and wasn't dialing the local police about a stranger on her doorstep. Max didn't need that headache on top of his continuing an investigation he'd been ordered to leave alone.

When the doorbell wasn't answered, Max knocked.

No response.

He knocked again, this time longer and harder.

Nothing.

Max looked toward the large window to his left. It was open and there were no shades or drapes blocking his view into the house. He moved closer, looking through the glass, knowing as he did something was very wrong. Summer O'Hara wanted to speak with him. She should have swung the door open the second he pulled into the drive. She hadn't struck Max as the kind of woman who would hide her enthusiasm for anything that spiked it. It was clear the

Flower of Scotland spiked Summer's enthusiasm.

Max scanned what looked to be a living room or some large sitting area. Neat. Clean. And empty. The kitchen lay beyond, and he couldn't see the entirety of it from where he stood. He looked to the staircase that wound up at an angle and ended directly about ten feet short of the front door.

The first thing Max saw after the tile at the base of stairs was a sandal. The slide in kind, without a back.

Then he saw a bare foot attached to a leg bent at an improbable angle.

He went to the door, knocked again, saying loudly, just in case the camera had an audio feature, "Federal agent," while turning the knob. He didn't pull his sidearm until he was through the front door. He went immediately to the woman. It was Summer O'Hara. No doubt about it, she looked just like the picture on her driver's license.

He swept the house, finding it empty. All the windows on the first and second story were open. Screens attached. No obvious sign of a break-in.

Max quickly made his way back to Summer. Her breathing was shallow, but steady. Her heartbeat slow, yet discernible. She was unresponsive when he called her name. Max kept his fingers at her neck, feeling her pulse as he said, "Ms. O'Hara, tell me what happened."

Max had found through trial and error that most people respond, or do their best to respond, if given a command rather than being asked a question.

"Summer, squeeze my hand if you can hear me," Max said, gently wrapping his hand around hers, letting his fingers touch her palm.

She responded with a feather light squeeze.

Emergency services would take close to an hour to get to Summer's house from Sturgeon Bay. Max passed a naturopathic clinic on his way from Fish Creek. He knew little about naturopaths other than they don't use herbs to cure emergency situations.

He did a quick inventory of Summer's injuries. He didn't want to wait for an ambulance—there wasn't time for that. Her left wrist may have been broken, but he didn't think her arm was. Her legs had the beginning of bruises but didn't look broken.

He stepped back, took a quick series of photos, then picked Summer O'Hara up and carried her to his car. The doorbell app caught it all on tape. No help for that. She needed medical attention and there didn't seem to be any obvious reason she was unresponsive to his questioning. There was no scent of alcohol on her, no bottle of pills spilled on the steps.

When he leaned down to pick her up, Summer moved. She was half sitting, half slouched, supporting her weight on her right arm.

She opened her eyes. "Drugged," she said. Not clearly, but Max understood.

She opened her opposite hand, which had been tightly clamped, revealing a small ring with a domed surface. "In the ring," Summer said. "Tea is in the ring."

Max put the ring in his pocket. "If I support you, can you make it to my car?"

Summer nodded.

Max lifted her under her arms, placed his shoulder under her left side, the side where her wrist was injured, and stood for a moment. Summer O'Hara leaned into him, giving him most of her weight. She was a small woman, maybe a buck twenty soaking wet. Her weigh didn't affect Max. "Let's see if you can walk."

She could but not well. He lifted her down the steps and kept her to his side until he reached the passenger side of his car.

Max took her straight to the back parking lot of the naturopathic clinic. Three things happened rapidly from there.

First, the naturopath knew immediately what had been given to Summer O'Hara in her tea from the sample Summer stored in her ring—a clever contraption that opened, revealing an inner compartment that sealed completely when closed.

Second, after diagnosing and treating Summer with the antidote, Summer formally died.

Third, Max sought and received, permission to investigate Jack Smith, not only for theft, money-laundering, and trafficking in stolen goods, but also for attempted murder, from his boss's boss. His investigation was eyes only, so no one on his team was advised. Max was simply relocated from Chicago to Milwaukee, where he needn't actually present himself.

It was the fourth thing that happened that would change Max Scott's life forever. He met the Murphy triplets—Summer O'Hara's children.

One knew his secret, which gave them a bond of sorts

and made liars of them both.

One he'd learn to tolerate but not before blood was shed.

One would prove to be to be his undoing.

CHAPTER TWO

Her mother was dead.

Fallon Murphy took the news first with shock, then with denial, and finally with an abject sorrow that left her numb. She and her brothers lost their father so young. Death didn't seem real then. Their father was there one day, then he went to work like always, then he was gone forever. Just like that.

Commercial fishermen on the Great Lakes took risks people not part of the industry didn't understand. The Great Lakes—massive bodies of fresh water—do not allow all who venture there to come home. To this day, every time Fallon stared out onto Lake Michigan, she felt her father's presence. She smelled his drugstore aftershave in the breeze off the water. She imagined her father's hand in hers when she ran her hand over the lake's cool surface. Fallon felt peace rather than sorrow when she was on the water. It didn't make sense to her that she felt whole on the water rather than fearful or angry. In the sentimentality of her heart, Fallon imagined that was her father's parting gift to his children.

They all loved the water.

It took years after losing their father for their mother to find love again. Geoff had been kind, funny, and so easy to love. He'd also been twenty years Summer's senior. When the housing market crashed in 2008 and the stock market followed, Geoff lost most of the capital he'd invested in both. He would have survived it; he certainly had the will and the knowledge to start over. Unfortunately, Geoff's heart had other ideas.

Losing two fathers had been hard on Fallon.

Losing her mother was unthinkable.

Fallon couldn't quite believe Summer was dead. Nothing about it felt right.

It didn't feel real. Not yet. Not when Fallon was so far away in a land so different from Door County, Wisconsin, yet so similar.

Life in Key West was lived in tune with the water. The same was true of Ephraim. One was less than one hundred miles from Cuba. The other had more in common with Canada than the tropics. Fallon escaped to Key West. Now, it was home. Going back to the Door for any extended period wasn't something Fallon thought she'd ever do. Under these circumstances, it sucked. That simple. That crude.

Her brother Gus called to give her the news. Ever the blunt one, he'd simply said, "You need to come home. Mom's dead. She's been cremated. The funeral is in three days." Four sentences. Gus turned her world upside down in fewer than twenty words.

When Fallon asked Gus what happened, all she got in response was a clipped, stoically brutal, "She slipped coming down the stairs. Then her heart just stopped beating. It was an accident, Fal. Just a tragic accident. Come home."

Fallon disconnected the call without asking who decided to have their mother cremated or why. Was her face that damaged that she couldn't have an open casket? Had mom changed her will adding the request to be cremated? Why wouldn't she be buried next to Geoff? Nothing made any sense. Fallon packed her one black dress, her heels, and a few odds and ends as she mindlessly made her way through her apartment. She hopped on the first nonstop flight to Milwaukee.

The first thing she planned to do when she made it home was hug her brother Fingal. The second thing she planned to do was punch Gus as hard as she possibly could. The third thing she would do was take her mother's ashes to the lake shore and sit with a bottle of Chardonnay. She wanted to watch the sunset with both her parents.

She'd cry when she made it back to her room in her mother's house. When she was alone. When she had the solitude, surrounded by her mother's things, to contemplate that in a very real sense she was now an orphan.

...

After Fallon arrived in Ephraim, she went directly to the funeral home to pick up her mother's ashes. She'd texted her brothers—both of them—with a statement that read more like an arrest warrant than a request. She wanted her mother's ashes, and she wanted them now. She'd have been nicer about it, but she discovered that they waited three days after Summer died to call her. They'd also made all the funeral arrangements without consulting her. She felt abandoned and angrier than she'd been when she left Ephraim.

She'd choked on the first sip of Chardonnay and abandoned it immediately.

While she felt the familiarity of her father as she sat on the lakeshore, throwing stones into the water as she'd done with her parents as a child, she didn't feel her mother's presence at all. That bothered her and made her angry. Fallon didn't want to cry. She wanted to rage against the proof sitting in the urn next to her. She felt like a crazy person, not a daughter grieving the loss of her mother.

Fallon heard the crunch of footsteps on the stones approaching her. She was in no mood for company, so she didn't look up. Didn't acknowledge the new arrival. She knew it wasn't one of her brothers. They both realized that she needed time before approaching her. While neither of them was overly intuitive, both valued their hides enough to let Fallon be until she was ready to walk with them.

The crunching stopped and a decidedly male presence plopped down beside her. He didn't say anything for a while. Letting Fallon get used to him, she supposed. Oddly enough she didn't care. He smelled of soap, salt, and a hint of lime. Similar to her father's aftershave but more elemental.

The next thing Fallon allowed herself to notice was his boat shoes. They were new. He wore them somewhat awkwardly, like they were foreign.

She heard him clink the bottle as it brushed against the stones. She heard the *pop* sound of the cork as he pulled it from the bottle. Then came the unmistakable sound of liquid pouring into plastic. Summer only carried plastic wineglasses outside, especially near the water, a habit Fallon picked up.

The stranger grabbed her hand where it wrapped around her upturned knees and thrust the over-sized rainbow-colored plastic wineglass into her hand. "Drink it," he demanded as if he had a right to demand anything from her. "It might not help, but odds are, it won't hurt."

Fallon took the glass, wondering why she felt comfortable taking it from a stranger. She thought she heard irony in his remark, or maybe it was commiseration. She didn't know him, so perhaps she was projecting more than she should. Maybe communing with a father she felt in the water and an urn that was supposed to be filled with her mother's ashes made one hyper-aware. Fallon hadn't known anyone with experience quite like hers to ask. She was losing it, self-aware enough to know she was on tenuous mental ground, but still losing it.

She should take the urn, the bottle, and high-tail it back to Summer's house and cry herself to sleep.

Instead of doing what she should, Fallon took a sip of her wine—which this time, tasted clean and crisp and welcoming—eyeing the man who poured it for her over the rim of her plastic glass. Eyes narrowing as he openly held her gaze.

His expression seemed more inquiring than merely affable, but perhaps that was the intelligence she thought she saw in his eyes. Eyes the color of the lake water where it hit the shore, magnifying the yellow, grey, and brown stones below—light greyish-blue with flecks of gold and brown to give them depth and interest. The dark ring around his irises only enhanced the lightness of his eyes.

The rest of him was well enough put together that she'd have approached him had he been dining alone at her restaurant. He appeared tall even though he was sitting. His shoulders were wide, but some of that was the way he held himself—straight back, chin up, chest out. He breathed from his diaphragm, which most people didn't. Fallon found that interesting and a little alarming. His face had character, like the men who frequented her restaurant in Key West. Most had stories they would never tell, not the real versions at least, but if you looked closely enough, you could see some of the joy, the fear, the will to re-invent written on the lines of their faces. Sometimes on their hands and arms as well.

Fallon took her time absorbing what she could from his appearance and demeanor.

He let her. He didn't rush or shy away from her scrutiny.

A man sure of whatever mission he was on. Fallon got the distinct impression that while she may be a part of that mission, she wasn't the center of it. He just wasn't giving off that kind of vibe.

Fallon set her wineglass down on the semi-flat rock to

her left. The man was to her right. No obstacles—save the urn and the partially filled Chardonnay bottle—between her and this dark-haired creature who wanted something from her. She was a black belt. She had little to lose. She was in a kick-tail-and-take-names kind of mood.

What was the worst that could happen?

Part of her wanted to find out.

Losing it, indeed.

Fallon looked at the compelling stranger, mentally measuring the distance between the bottle and the rock. "Which are you: law enforcement, military, or ex-military?"

When he flinched, a tiny jerk he controlled quickly, Fallon knew he was one of the above. She cut the pretense of civility and said, "You are uncomfortable in your shoes."

Fallon gritted her teeth and edged closer to the bottle. "You sit up straight." When doubt or something like confusion flashed in his eyes, Fallon continued through gritted teeth, "You have a military bearing."

He gave nothing away except the tick at his jaw and the hardening of his welcoming eyes.

"You breathe through your abdomen, and you scan the horizon for every threat and every means of escape. You're good at making it appear nonchalant, but you're scanning, not mindlessly enjoying your environment."

His jaw hardened.

Fallon edged closer to the bottle. She was now equal distance between the rock and the bottle. She may have a struggle on her hands, but she'd make him bleed if she had too. Nothing in his demeanor so far hinted at aggression toward her, but she'd be a fool not to be aware of the fact that he was capable of it.

An iron grip came down on her wrist before Fallon even knew she was grabbing for the bottle.

"Don't even think about it," he said before nuzzling her neck as he whispered in her ear, "I am not your enemy." To anyone watching, they'd see an intimate moment. Two lovers enjoying the lakeshore.

He held Fallon close as she struggled.

"Don't fight me, Fallon. I'll make sure you direct all that homicidal energy in the right direction." He paused a beat, then said, "Trust me."

His voice was calm.

Decisive.

Immediately trustworthy.

His grip was strong and firm. He wasn't hurting her. He was constraining her. She hated it. The second she stopped fighting him, he let her go.

"Who are you?" Fallon asked, looking up into those compelling eyes.

He stared down at her almost sternly but not quite making it happen, begging her to believe him.

"The man who knows where your mother is."

...

She took one look at him and knew he was full of shit.

The second Max sat down next to Fallon, he knew he was out of his league. She didn't startle. She didn't move away. She didn't accept his presence, but she didn't tell him to buzz off either. She sat there, eyed him up and down,

and came to conclusions—most of which were spot on—
before he opened his mouth.

Max's excitement at getting close to the team who stole
the Flower of Scotland made his blood burn through his
veins. He felt it like a tangible warmth since he carried
Summer O'Hara into Julie Grace's naturopathic clinic. Dr.
Grace, the naturopath with grit and sass, saved Summer's
life. Max had no doubt about that. She knew what to give
Summer to counteract the plant poison put into her tea.

Then Dr. Grace went five steps further. She agreed to
produce a death certificate—Max's off-the-books FBI
contacts helped with that. His father lent him most of the
cash he needed since it couldn't be requisitioned through
formal FBI channels. Max had been assured his father—a
retired FBI veteran—would be reimbursed, so long as both
Max and his father, Roland Scott, kept all the receipts.

Roland, aka "Rolly" Scott, had no qualms about
jumping back into the fray to help his son. In fact, he
seemed giddy about it. Some of that was seeing photos of
Summer O'Hara in the briefing materials Max sent to him.

Summer O'Hara was a beautiful woman. The
combination of red hair and blue eyes that happened rarely
in nature defined her facial features. It didn't hurt that she
kept herself in good shape, or that she inherited good bone
structure. But that was the two-dimensional woman.
Summer was far more attractive in person than photos
could capture.

The intelligence in her eyes, her quick wit and easy
smile, even knowing she'd been targeted by a man bent on
ensuring her silenced, made her just the kind of woman his

father couldn't ignore—smart, engaging, and teasingly sarcastic. Something about that combination pushed every one of Rolly Scott's buttons. Didn't hurt that she had red hair. Two of Rolly's ex-wives had red hair. Neither lasted long, but that didn't stop his father from trying to make one stick.

Max's mother, who died when Max was seventeen, had been kind, funny, sardonic—a trait Max associated with intelligence to this day. She also had red hair and blue eyes. Rolly wasn't the only Scott male who had a soft spot for women who resembled Max's mother, both inside and out. Max liked Summer instantly. He'd do anything he could to protect her. Since he knew Rolly would put Summer's safety above his own, he trusted his father to keep her safe.

The fewer people who knew Summer was alive, the better. Right now, that list was manageable: his boss's boss, Dr. Grace and her fiancé—who was also her assistant and had access to just about anything legal and quasi-legal, Summer's son Gus or Fergus—because Max needed help making funeral arrangements without a body, and now his dad.

Max had to make a choice: tell Fallon and enlist her help, or keep her and her other brother, Fingal, in the dark. Their reactions would be more authentic if he and Gus allowed them to stay in the dark.

If Max told them their mother was alive, the risk to his case escalated.

If he allowed them to continue to believe their mother was dead, he'd do damage to his soul. He'd have given anything to believe his mother was still alive, to save himself and his father the pain that still filled them both.

There was also the fact that Summer was safer if her children thought she was dead. Two of them anyway. He could mitigate the risk to Summer. He and his father knew how. What they couldn't fix was the sense of betrayal that would plague Summer and her children for the rest of their lives if they didn't come clean as soon as possible.

Max wasn't willing to tear apart a family simply to make a case—not when odds were good that he and Rolly could keep Summer O'Hara safely guarded. Odds weren't quite as good that they could keep the triplets safe without enlisting their help. Help required trust. Lying never served Max well when it came to building trust. He made a habit of keeping his lies to a minimum.

That had the added benefit of not have to remember them. Stick to the truth as far as you're able. Truth may not set you free, but it will keep you safer than the alternative. Purely a matter of playing the odds. That's what his first undercover training had taught him. It had served Max well over the years.

Until he sat down next to Fallon Murphy.

She sucked every good intention from him and left him thinking thoughts he had no business thinking. The first of which made absolutely no sense to him. *Protect her at all costs...keep her by your side...*

Max shot that line of thinking so fast his teeth hurt with the effort. How was he going to get her to trust him when he didn't trust himself?

She took one look at him and knew he was a fraud. A fake. A man uncomfortable in his shoes. How in the heck had she nailed that with a look? So much for his undercover skills. He'd blown it by wearing what every overpaid boat owner in Door County wore.

Max didn't know what to expect from Fallon. A light flirtation, a quick buzz-off, a polite "Please leave me alone." He hadn't expected Fallon to try to brain him with a half-filled Chardonnay bottle. He probably should have. Had someone like him sat down next to him while he was mourning, he'd have warned them off *impolitely*, and if they didn't high-tail it fast enough, he would have *politely* punched them in the face.

In a few days he had to study Fallon, her brothers, and Mr. Jack Smith, high-end boutique jeweler and master thief. He'd learned the Murphy siblings were all hard-working, life-loving, hard-headed individuals who had no issue demanding what they wanted out of life and fighting to get it. The brothers, Max understood. Fallon, he couldn't figure out.

She didn't make sense.

Graduated in the top quarter of her high school. Good, but not stellar. Did better in undergraduate school, studying history, philosophy, and comparative literature. Odd mix, but there it was. Then, she nailed her LSATs and went to law school. There she graduated in the top ten percent of her class. She spent two years at the top criminal defense firm, and then, when she was just establishing her reputation as a litigator, respected by her colleagues and the district attorneys who worked opposite her, she disappeared.

Max hadn't been able to track her movements until she

surfaced in Key West. Older. More sophisticated, not less. And running a restaurant that locals and tourists frequented. Most of them with secrets. A place where deals were made and money was exchanged with the frequency of bottles of Land Shark at the bar.

She had no ties to criminality. None.

But the man who employed her walked a fine line on both sides of the good citizen aisle. Law enforcement monitored but did little more because Nick Card threw them a bad guy on a semi-regular basis—often enough to maintain his usefulness. Nick Card had his own sense of integrity. It wasn't close to Max's definition of the word, but it was honorable in its own way. What didn't make sense was Fallon's connection to any of it. Maybe, if he worked at it, he'd get a glimpse into what made her tick.

The light in her eyes made him want to try.

"Trust me," he said to Fallon as he held her close.

"Who are you?" she asked.

"I'm the man who knows where your mother is."

And he did.

"Let me show you."

CHAPTER THREE

The orchard Gus managed with his brother, Fingal, was thriving. They'd had another hard winter which hadn't helped the cherry production, but somehow the newer trees they planted were still growing strong. The heavy, wet snowfall they had throughout the Door in late April put them behind schedule. That late, unexpected snow put every farmer in Wisconsin behind schedule, so that, in and of itself, wouldn't hinder the cherry crop.

What worried Gus about the winery, orchard, and gallery wasn't the late spring or the early dry summer; it was the lie he kept. It was eating him alive. That lie when it came out, and come out it would, would damage his relationship with his sister past the underlying strain that already existed. Letting Finn believe their mother was dead would earn him a bloody nose and, best case, a summer of barely civil mutual détente—their personal Cold War in which mutually assured destruction ruled their every interaction.

His siblings were stubborn. They held grudges. They

loved deeply but forgave one another only when forgiveness was earned. Gus certainly had earned their ire. He couldn't think of one way to earn either's forgiveness.

Gus carried the case of semi-dry red Finn had asked him to get for the tasting bar from the storage house in the back. They were running low on their bestselling red. That had Finn concerned. He didn't want to lose customer base due to lack of product. There were just too many great red wine choices in their twelve to fifteen-dollar price to alienate even one consistent customer.

"We're down to twenty-four cases of the Fallon Red," Gus said. Finn had his back to him, stocking the side bar with small tasting glasses.

"We'll have to start pushing the new Rosé. Twenty-four cases won't get us through August." Finn's voice was dull. Matter-of-fact. Monotone. Like he knew he was saying the right thing but couldn't quite make himself believe it.

The Rosé was a Murphy Brother's original. Their first original was their semi-dry red with the punch of Pinot Noir mixed with the smoothness of a full Cabernet. They named that one after their sister and it was an immediate success. So much so, they couldn't keep up with demand.

They named their Rosé after their mother: *Summer Rose Rosé.*

In the blind tastings they'd had so far, Summer Rose outshined both the California Rosé they stocked and the Oregon variety. They had another winner, and neither Finn nor Fallon felt good about serving it. Finn couldn't do it without getting sullen and misty-eyed, something no barkeep could do without losing every customer who approached the counter.

Gus couldn't stand anymore what circumstance made him do. He didn't like the sense of betrayal it made him feel. He didn't even like looking in the mirror when he brushed his teeth. This necessary farce couldn't end fast enough for him. He could have just killed Jack Smith and been done with it, but that FBI agent wasn't sure Smith was the one who tried to kill Summer. He'd also planted the idea that if—and Special Agent Max Scott had stressed the *if*—Jack Smith had poisoned Summer and pushed her down her stairs, he probably hadn't acted alone.

Gus opened the case of Fallon Red with so much force, he rendered it unusable. He stopped. Stood up straight, rubbed a palm across his forehead, then through hair already mussed from the repeated act. "I'm going out," he said.

Finn turned to finally look at him. "Where are you going? There's still more stocking to do, and we haven't gone over the new labels yet."

Gus was already walking away. "Get Sully to stock. The answer on the labels can wait. If you don't think so, pick one. I don't really care anymore."

Finn's accusation followed him out the door, "You don't care about anything or anyone other than yourself anymore."

What hurt more than Finn's words echoing through Gus's brain was the certainty that when his siblings discovered their mother was alive they'd believe those words were true. Gus knew, in the dark part of his soul, that they were true.

His need to keep their mother safe obliterated his duty to his siblings because he couldn't live with himself if anything more happened to her when he could have stopped it. He should have insisted Summer stay with him after their encounter with Smith. He should have cared more about her and less about trying to bail out the gallery, keep the orchard thriving, and the shop under control.

He was feeling miserable, self-absorbed, and sick to his stomach for making this about him and not about Summer.

Gus had no idea where he would end up when he got on his Sportster and turned left onto Highway 42. But he should have known better not to stop riding until he got his self-absorbed temper under control. Anger, fear, and a sprinkling of stupid had never served him well.

Today was no exception to that rule.

Gus didn't know that today's little excursion to the dark side would put them all in more danger than he could have imagined.

. . .

Fallon looked at the man who claimed to know where her mother was with all the jaded hope she could muster. She wanted to believe him almost as much as she needed to. She sure as the day was long in Door County in the summer, never truly believed the urn next to her contained what remained of her mother. Not overtly religious in theory, Fallon was deeply spiritual in practice. Since she was a little girl, Fallon believed God lived in her. She'd grown to rely on what her inner self told her with matters of the heart and soul.

Her mother lived in her heart and her soul. She still felt her there in a way that was definitely corporal, not otherworldly.

"Tell me your name," Fallon demanded. "I'm going to scream bloody murder if you don't tell me your real name right bloody now."

He laughed, touching the side of her face gently with the back of his hand before he folded both arms over his knees. If he was trying to appear harmless, he was failing spectacularly, but with flare.

"You certainly say 'bloody' a lot."

Fallon flushed. That was true. But only when she felt off her game in a way that left the façade of control over her environment in ashes. Her eyes flashed to the ornate urn beside her. This time the ashes were literal. Summer would have hated the urn. Fallon had no idea what her brothers were thinking picking it. It was etched with white calla lilies. Flamboyantly floral. Gus and Finn would have done better with dandelions. There was a resilient bloom her mother would have approved of.

The absurdity of her thoughts brought a small smile to Fallon's face. The smile had the added benefit of grounding her. She no longer wanted to throw the word "bloody" into every sentence.

"Max," the stranger said. "My name is Max."

"Is that your real name?"

"Yes. Maxwell Scott is my full name. I work for the FBI. I'm part of the Jewelry and Gem Theft Team." He shrugged and cocked his head to one side as he scrutinized her reaction. Nothing in his demeanor nor tone suggested he was being anything but honest with her. "However, *team* might be a bit of a stretch on this one. My team thinks I've been canned. Probably would have been, too, had it not been for your mother."

"Bloody hell. You're telling the truth," Fallon said, believing him.

He smiled fully at her, meeting her eyes with real warmth. The effect was instantaneously devastating to Fallon's overwhelmed senses. She felt lighter than she'd felt since Gus's phone call—like a real weight had been lifted from her chest. She felt like invisible strings were pulling her up and nothing would weigh her down. Light as air. Buoyant even. "Take me to my mother."

Max reached into his shirt pocket and pulled out a thin, white-gold diamond eternity band. "Give me your hand."

When Fallon took too long trying to determine what she should do, Max reached out and grabbed her left hand. He slid the band over her ring finger. It fit perfectly. Since Fallon's hands were relatively small, that was almost as surprising as the ring itself.

Fallon looked at the ring on her finger.

Then she looked up into Max's eyes, guarded now, and expectant, like there was another shoe getting ready to drop right on Fallon's head. She fitted what he was saying into an unfinished puzzle in her head.

FBI. Jewelry Theft. Summer O'Hara—jewel and jewelry lover needing to appear dead. Wedding band on her finger.

Fallon swallowed past the lump in her throat. "Take me to my mother. You can explain about the ring and everything else on the way."

Max grabbed her left hand and brought it to his lips. His voice was low and gravelly when he spoke. "When we get up from the beach we will be married. I'm here to help you settle your mother's estate. We are living temporarily in Summer's house until we can get things settled. I know this is a lot to take in, but you're going to have to step up and make it happen. My case depends upon it. Your mother's safety depends on my case."

He paused, looking at her like he was willing her to get with the program. And pretty darned quick.

"My name—the name you will use for me—is Max Smart. I'm a business analyst. I help large companies stay large and up-and-coming companies grow. I travel often for business but have a few weeks downtime to help you and your family get Summer's things in order. We are recently married. We met six months ago when I came to your restaurant to meet Nick Card and help him with a new business acquisition. We had instant chemistry. We fell in love quickly and since we're both over thirty, saw no reason not to marry. You kept your maiden name. We were about to tell your family and arrange for a small ceremony here in Door County when the news arrived about the death of your mother."

Max rattled all that off with the quick efficiency Fallon associated with law enforcement. Lines of a story pieced together to make an outline of a whole while completely ignoring emotional content that made any tale real.

"Do I have your cooperation?" Max asked.

Fallon wasn't sure what Max meant by "cooperation."

What he seemed determined to take from her was absolute acquiescence to everything he demanded. *That* would never happen. He'd learn that about his "wife" very quickly. Just not before Fallon saw her mother.

"You have my *help* with your case. You have my *demand* that I see my mother, right bloody now." Fallon took a deep breath and let him see the truth of what she was about to say in her eyes. "You have my *promise* that if any more harm comes to my mother as a result of your investigation, that *I* will hold you, Maxwell Scott Smart, totally responsible, and *I* will exact my pound of flesh directly from your hide."

He had the audacity to grin. "Are you threatening bodily harm to a federal agent?"

"You bet your bloody hide I am."

"We really have to do something about your choice of words."

And just like that, Fallon Murphy went from being a *me* to a *we*.

CHAPTER FOUR

Summer O'Hara had vague memories of being carried into Julie Grace's medical clinic by a disconcertingly strong and equally compelling young man who appeared to be older than her triplets but still young enough to be her son. The man had a nice voice. The problem was he used it incessantly.

She just wanted to go to sleep.

He kept moving her and shaking her and talking at her until she acknowledged him.

Then Julie and her assistant, Peter, pumped her stomach, made her drink more water than one mortal human could possibly flush through their system, and they made her drink a chalky tea that tasted like salty seaweed. If she lived through this, which Peter insisted she would while he helped her to the restroom for the eleventh time, she was never going to willingly drink that wretched tea again.

By the time she could have a coherent conversation that didn't involve asking for soda crackers or lotioned toilet paper, the FBI agent who saved her life had her ensconced on a mini-yacht with an older version of himself. Same devastating smile. Half the charm. The man was an overbearing nightmare.

And Summer was locked on a boat with him while they made their way along Lake Michigan's coast from Ephraim to his condo on the river in Milwaukee.

Rolly…his name was Rolly. What kind of name was Rolly? It sounded like some old-time baseball player with a handlebar mustache, or an eight-year-old boy who hadn't quite grown into his name. Because he insisted everyone call him Rolly, Summer refused to. It was one of the few things she could control about her life now. As an added bonus, it made him grit his teeth when Summer needed to call him by his name: *Roland*. When she was put out with him, which was anytime he took away her iPad, cell phone, or laptop, Summer rolled the *R* in his name dramatically.

She was now a woman unconnected. That was making her want to climb the walls even more than having no one to talk to who didn't want to dictate her every move. It was bad enough she needed to hide; it was worse she had a keeper who wouldn't so much as allow her to view the online jewelry sites she loved. Summer was a reader as well as a surfer. She loved to read e-books on her iPad. Roland would not allow that.

He did cave in and let her read her morning papers from his computer. He had online subscriptions to the *New York Times, Wall Street Journal,* and *Business Journal.* He caved further and added the *Washington Post, Boston Globe,* and *Guardian.* Roland also had a nice collection of hardcovers and paperbacks, most of which she hadn't read. He had the full spectrum of James Lee Burke, Clive Cussler, and Lee Child. But he also had books by Terry Pratchett, Ursula Le Guin—including one on writing—and a trio of old historical romance novels set in Scotland by Julie Garwood. Interesting choice for a man as masculine as Rolly Scott. There was also a selection on environmental conservation, books about adventure travel, and *The Hidden Life of Trees*.

For a man of such eclectic tastes in reading material, *Roland* had one persona. All-protective-alpha-male—all the time. Summer wasn't allowed to frequent any of the sites she generally frequented online, except for her newspapers. His overabundance of caution made her want to howl at the moon and break into his stash of single malt whisky and top shelf bourbon.

Summer took off her sandals. She didn't like them anyway. They chaffed. What she needed was a good pair of walking sandals she could get wet and a good pair of boat shoes. She'd never been a fan of boat shoes, but if she was going to be held captive on a boat, she might as well look like she belonged here. She sure didn't feel like she did.

She hadn't set foot on any boat, not even a kayak, since her first husband's death. Padraig—or Patrick, or sometimes simply Murph—had been a commercial fisherman. The lake had taken her first love, the father of her children. Summer still loved the water, almost as much as she still had the irrepressible fire of first love in her heart, but she didn't love boats or ships or whitefish the way she used to. In fact, she hadn't had a Door County fish boil since the last one she'd had at the White Gull Inn with

Padraig. His sister had made the trip from Galway, Ireland, and wanted the authentic Door County experience. Padraig had smiled and made sure she got the royal treatment. Then he'd snuck into the kitchen where his mate had a porterhouse waiting for him.

The thought made her smile. Padraig hated fish boils. Give the man a good steak and he was happy. Serve him the fruits of the sea—or lake—and odds were he'd be grumbling all night while waiting to eat something with hooves. The man didn't even like potatoes unless they were french-fried.

"What has you smiling so sweetly?" Rolly asked, coming to sit on the couch next to Summer. Lifting her bare feet, he sat down next to her, then placed her feet on his lap. The action wasn't threatening. Rolly acted like it was something he did all the time. Still, it felt intimate to Summer. She hadn't been touched by a man in a long time. The casual intimacy burned her to her core but didn't seem to affect him in the slightest.

Summer hoped her feet didn't stink. She didn't want to encourage Max's father. He already asked too many probing questions, but she didn't really want to repulse the man either.

"Shouldn't you be manning the deck or whatever else a captain has to do on his boat?" she asked, setting down *The Bride*. It was one of three Julie Garwood books Roland had on his shelf, secured by an ingenious yet simple system of elastic and Velcro.

Roland absently started to rub her ankles. He was good at it. Since he didn't seem to put any meaning into it at all and since it felt good, Summer let him continue. She'd been told she carried much of her tension in her feet the few times she'd gone for therapeutic massages. Summer was fairly certain being poisoned and pushed down the stairs had caused more tension to accumulate in all sorts of places.

"We're anchored for the night. We've got time before dinner. I thought we could talk or watch a movie. Maybe play some cards." Roland smiled at her. It was a light, teasing smile. The same one that took her off guard and put her at ease at the same time. It was the kind of smile a woman could learn to love, waking up to it every morning for the rest of her life.

Summer shut the book. She had no business reading romance. Apparently, it did funny things to her head. She did manage to bookmark her page with the worn jacket cover before closing it. Summer narrowed her eyes at Roland hoping he'd just go away. Or at least stop smiling at her.

As if he were reading her thoughts, his smile widened, making the lines at the corners of his eyes deepen. Roland Scott was an attractive man. No doubt about that. He also had the kind of confidence that came with age and experience. He didn't seem to care about his appearance; he was simply comfortable and confident in who he was. As dictatorial as he'd been about Summer staying out of sight and doing everything he told her to do before they left port in Ephraim, now he was more relaxed.

More open.

More compelling.

Summer felt like she was making a friend, that kind of tentative feeling of making friends before becoming a teenager and everything became about sex. It was a nice feeling. Roland was a nice man when he chose to be.

"Are you going to tell me why you were smiling when I came down? You looked lost in a memory. Judging by the far off look in your eye, it was a good one." Roland's voice was light, as if treading gently on the surface of getting to know her. Still, he seemed genuinely interested, and Summer couldn't think of one reason not to tell him. She wasn't secretive by nature or inclination which is exactly what got her into the predicament she was currently in. Had she just kept her suspicions to herself about the Zoe Tiara and the Flower of Scotland, she'd be safely ensconced in her own bed right now.

Alone.

"I was thinking about my first husband, Padraig Yeats Murphy," Summer said. Simply saying Padraig's full name aloud made Summer smile.

"Yeats?" Roland asked with genuine curiosity.

Summer snorted. She couldn't help it. Yeats was a ridiculous name to attach to someone like her first husband. Summer looked into Roland's light blue eyes, enjoying his company. He had a way of putting her at ease that she didn't fight. She needed the ease, something she hadn't felt in a very long time. "Padraig's mother loved Yeats. She'd often say, 'Watch how you walk through this world. Tread lightly, for you tread on my dreams.'"

Roland seemed to ponder that. He said nothing, simply waiting for her to continue or not. It was up to her.

Summer appreciated that. Another thing in her life she had control of—her story.

"I think I fell in love with her before I fell in love with Padraig. Padraig had his mother's poetic soul but none of her culinary preferences. He was a commercial fisherman who hated the taste of fish." Summer laughed. "And a first-generation Irishman who hated potatoes." Summer's brow furrowed as her smile deepened. "What kind of Irishman doesn't like fish and potatoes?"

Roland smiled with her. "What did he like?"

"Red meat, teaching his babies rebel songs, and …"

Summer's voice trailed off as she looked away from him. Rolly wanted to see her eyes light with love and the softness of good memories again. He'd seen her fired up and full of sass. He'd seen the fear as they pulled out of port and into open water. He'd seen the loneliness when she thought he wasn't looking. He'd seen that look often enough in his own reflection not to notice it in a kindred soul. Part of him hoped he could banish that particular demon from both their souls—for at least a while.

"*And…*" Rolly urged Summer to continue.

She looked him straight in the eyes, as if she could see straight through to the heart of him with those clear blue eyes of hers, and said, "Me." She swallowed hard and those lovely eyes grew misty. "He liked me."

Me too, he wanted to say. Because it was true. Rolly liked Summer O'Hara more than he should, although he didn't try to hard not to. Summer was easy to like. He hadn't liked a woman like he liked Summer in more years than he could count. Now that he was retired, golfing, writing, and sailing simply hadn't filled him the way they used to. He wanted a friend. Not the man kind he'd have a beer with after eighteen holes, but the woman kind he could tell secrets to while rubbing her feet.

Retiring had a way of realigning priorities. It also was offering him a chance to redefine who and what he wanted to be.

Wanting to banish the mist and bring back the mellowness Summer had shown before, Rolly nodded toward the hardcover set on the table. "That belonged to my second wife."

Summer sat up a bit straighter, but she didn't pull her feet from him.

"You kept your second wife's books? How many wives have you had?"

Ah, he thought. That was better. A little give and take as far as their romantic histories went and genuine female interest as evidence by the multiple questions—the latter of which was the more important of the two. He would have smiled at how easily he'd led her where he wanted her to go, but Summer seemed truly interested. He'd also learned she didn't have pretense in her. If she wanted something, she asked. If she was angry, she showed it. Clearly and without obfuscation. Summer didn't hide what she was thinking or how she felt. Rolly wasn't sure he could handle Summer O'Hara, but surprisingly he wanted to try.

She'd been honest with him. He found, again to his surprise, that not only did he want to answer her questions about him, he wanted her to keep asking.

"Yes," he answered nodding to the other two books in

the series still on the shelf. "I kept those three. I considered them hazard pay after they were thrown at my head."

Summer was gearing up to ask more about that. He could tell by the flash of amused interest in her widened eyes. He stopped her by answering her second question. "Three. I've had three wives." His eyes narrowed of their own volition for a millisecond, and his hand involuntarily stilled its gentle exploration of Summer's ankle. "I would have had only one had Max's mother not passed."

"I'm sorry," Summer said, meaning it.

How often he'd heard those exact words over the years. Not once before now had they brought him any kind of comfort. Summer was sorry he didn't get to finish the life he'd laid out for himself on his wedding day. She hadn't been able to finish hers either. Only she'd had that particular pain not once, but twice.

"It was a long time ago. Max was already a man—or nearly so. Peggy was healthy one day, sick the next, and gone twelve weeks later."

"I'm sure she'd never have left you or Max if she'd have had a choice."

No one had said that to him before. His other two wives had left him. He hadn't given them much of a choice. Truth be told, had they not, he would have left them.

Summer surprised him by changing direction entirely. Rolly gave a self-deprecating snort at her next question.

"So, you kept your second wife's books because they made good projectile weapons?" she asked smiling sideways at him. That teasing smile hinted at the girl she had been. Only the crinkles at the edges of her eyes and bracketing her smile belied her age. A fact Rolly found vastly appealing.

"That was an added bonus."

The head cock got more pronounced as the grin dimmed to a warm smile. "Why keep the books? They don't seem like the kind of books a man like you would keep."

Rolly was curious to hear what kind of man Summer thought he was, beyond the obvious. But he was willing to wait until he showed her more of himself before he heard her assessment of him. He did raise a brow at her comment. When she kept smiling at him, he resumed his gentle stroking of her ankles. Trying to keep it light. Offhanded. Like he wasn't even aware of the heat radiating from her directly into him.

"She loved those books. I read them and a handful of others in an attempt to get closer to her." He shrugged. None of it even hurt anymore, although he felt a stab of regret that he hadn't tried harder to make either one of his marriages work after Peggy. "I kept the books I enjoyed. Tossed the ones I didn't."

"What did you like about these books," Summer asked, truly interested. She'd never met a man who read romance on purpose. Certainly not one who's motivation was to get closer to someone he loved.

"I like the spunk, the strength, and the seemingly eternal optimism of the female characters. And the fact that after terrorizing them, they forgive their heroes."

Summer laughed. What a fabulous reason to read. And an even better reason to keep old stories. "Rolly Scott, you are a sentimental soul."

Rolly grinned at her. He was nothing of the sort. He had managed to get Summer O'Hara to use the name he preferred which pleased him almost as much as a kiss would have. *Small steps, Rolly. Small, careful steps. Tread lightly…for you tread on your dreams.*

"I'm a practical soul, dear lady. And keep what brings me joy." Let her make of that what she would. "How about a glass of Rosé while we play cribbage? I have on good authority the wine I stocked is named after you," Rolly said as he moved her legs to the side and stood. He immediately missed touching her, but he wanted more stories from her, and card and drink had a way of bringing them out in most people.

Summer sat up, letting her feet fall to the floor. She eyed his liquor cabinet. "Make that two fingers Four Roses neat and you've got yourself a deal."

"Done," Rolly said.

And just like that, a friendship that would last the rest of their natural lives began.

CHAPTER FIVE

It was a beautiful afternoon. The breeze off the lake was gentle, adding a crispness to the otherwise warm air. The sky was blue, filled with patches of translucent white clouds. The songs of robins and wrens, sparrows and finches, and soft cooing of doves filled the air away from the water and the distant sounds of motor boats.

The air smelled fresh and new, like it did every summer after the cherry blossoms fell. Tulips and daffodils bloomed. A myriad of summer annuals perfumed the air from planting boxes and baskets that filled every inch of available space not reserved for trees and manicured lawns.

Fallon found it odd how much she loved Door County in the summertime, how peaceful it was even with the constant buzz of tourists milling everywhere. She had a million and one questions reverberating through her head as she and Max made their way from the shore to Summer's home. So many in fact, she couldn't pick one.

Part of that may have been the fact that Max was holding her hand while they walked. Naturally they seemed to fall into step with one another. Like breathing. It took no effort; it just flowed. Step by step in tune. Holding Max's hand felt right. Reassuring. Like she could count on him. While none of that made logical sense, Fallon wouldn't deny the truth of it. Denial had never served her well in the past, so she'd made a concerted effort not to allow herself to indulge in its dangerous depths.

They were just approaching her mother's favorite jewelry shop when Fallon heard the familiar rumble of Gus's 2010 Harley CRD XR 1200. Harley launched the bike only in Europe. It had cost Gus a small fortune to have it crated over from Spain. There was only one motorcycle in the Door like it and it was Gus's.

One look at Gus as he parked it in Jack Smith's small parking lot next to the jewelry store, and all Fallon saw was red. By the time Gus was taking off his Shoe full-face helmet, she was ready to take him to the ground. She may have too, if Max hadn't held her back.

He clamped down on her hand as she tried to cross the road. There was only one main route in and out of Ephraim, and it was busy throughout the tourist season. On a clear day like today, it was dangerously busy. "Calm down," Max hissed in her ear. "He's seen you. If that pale look on his face is any indication, he knows you're angry. Anger has no place here for either of you. I need you to put a lid on it and pretty damned fast."

He smiled at her through gritted teeth. "Smith is coming out of his shop. Follow my lead or risk Summer never being able to go outside again without looking over her shoulder for her would-be killer."

Max didn't wait for Fallon to answer. He started waving instead like a joyful madman at Gus. He shouted across to Fallon's perplexed brother. "Hey, Gus, thanks for meeting me, Bro. I hadn't counted on your sister being with us."

A weak smile grew on Gus's face as he slowly waved back. "Got here as quickly as I could," he said, falling into his role as follower of Max's lead.

Max crossed the road at the first clearing between slow moving, yet consistent traffic. He made his way to Gus and enveloped him in what looked to be a painful hug. "You're here *early*. I wanted this to be a surprise for your sister."

"Oh, she looks plenty surprised," Gus said, making Fallon wonder if she was the only one who noticed the sardonic and worried edge to his upbeat tone. Probably. She was sensitive to it in a way even the triplets' best friends growing up hadn't noticed.

Jack Smith made his way down the concrete steps in front of his front door. "Been kind of slow here today, gentlemen. What can I help you with," he asked amicably enough, although Fallon thought she saw a calculating shrewdness in his eyes that had little to do with how close he could come to his three-hundred percent markup.

Max turned toward Jack Smith and switched into a different person. He was warm and engaging and effusing. He didn't even look the same. Gone were the penetrating and assessing eyes. Now those eyes said everyone he met was destined to be his best friend and wasn't he just so happy to be part of that experience. The transformation was uncanny.

The smile Max sent Fallon was loving and gentle and

filled with a knowing sensuality that said he wanted to hold her to him naked forever. Fallon's throat went dry as he pulled her to his side. "I was going to surprise my bride with a belated engagement ring, but this oaf came early, before I could get his sister home. He was going to help me pick out something wonderful. Now that the cat's out of the bag, I guess Gus's help is no longer needed."

Max turned to face Gus and his smile deepened. Only this time it didn't reach his eyes. Gus got the message. He smiled, too. Then he slapped Max's shoulder. As a gesture of brotherly competition couched in brotherly love, it managed to look real enough. Gus still couldn't meet Fallon's eyes, though. He hastily put on his helmet after he said to Max, "Meet you guys up at Mom's in about an hour. I'll grab Finn. He's expecting dinner and drinks on the back deck."

Gus was backing up the Sportster as Max said, "Take your time. You're in charge of the wine. Steaks are in the fridge."

Gus waved, started his bike and was gone without once looking Fallon in the eye. Fallon tamped down her anger. Max was right. With Jack Smith watching every nuance, this was neither the time nor the place to tip their hand.

Jack's gaze shifted from Max to Fallon. They'd met before. Summer managed to drag her into his shop at least once a summer when Fallon visited. They hadn't exchanged more than a dozen or so words. Her mother was the one who loved to talk jewelry. That didn't stop Jack Smith's probing words or assessing eyes. "I was sorry to hear about your mother, Fallon." He cocked his head at her and leaned down. He was a tall man, taller than her, playing at comfort by leaning in, waiting to see if she'd jerk back.

She didn't. In fact, she smiled a small sad, detached smile. Men as trained in their craft as Jack Smith had tried to play her for any number of reasons over a period of years. Her boss, and the one man she called friend, Nick Card, had taught her how to recognize their tells. She knew how to use them to her advantage, while never once giving away by word, deed, or micro-expression what she was feeling. The trick she'd learned was not to feel, to take herself out of the moment and replace herself with whomever the men assumed her to be.

"Thank you, Mr. Smith," she said, holding his gaze for a moment before looking down. Her voice was softer when she continued, "It's been a difficult time for my brothers and me. Especially for Gus. He's as angry about losing our mom as he is hurt. It makes him impulsive."

"I'm surprised you'd be shopping for an engagement ring at a time like this," Jack said neutrally, his gaze shifting between Fallon and Max.

Fallon wrapped her arm around Max's and pulled him closer into her. She looked up into his face and smiled her best *You-walk-on-water-and-I'll-love-you-forever* smile at him. She toned the smile down a bit but kept it in place as she looked toward Jack Smith. "This wasn't my idea, Mr. Smith. I'm perfectly happy with my wedding band. I'm not the jewelry lover my mother was…" Fallon let her voice trail off.

Max picked it up beautifully. He tapped her arm with his free hand. "That's why this is the perfect time to pick out a ring, love. We'll be honoring your mother's love of jewelry. You'll get to pick out something perfect from her favorite shop. Every time you look at it, you'll have a good memory of your mom and a loving memory of me."

Well, after that load of sentimental—yet convincingly sincere—horse manure, not even someone as slick as Jack Smith could suggest it wasn't the ideal time to buy solidified carbon, compressed over millennia in the earth's crust.

"Shall we," Max asked gesturing toward the stairs that led to Jack Smith's jewelry shop.

Fallon smiled at him, enjoying herself, despite the fact that she may have just engaged pleasantries with her mother's would-be killer. Maybe she was enjoying herself because of it. Either way, she'd take pleasure in taking the man down.

"We shall," Fallon said, stepping once again in perfect time with Max and following Jack Smith, wherever that caging criminal chose to lead.

...

Gus's little intervention had forced Max into Jack Smith's shop before he was ready. But now that he was there, Max was determined not to leave until he scoped out every jewel in the place. As it turned out, Jack Smith led Max and Fallon to the case farthest from the front door that held vintage diamond rings. Not a Harry Winston, Cartier, Graff, or a Van Cleef and Arpels, among them. Max spotted an older Tiffany piece from about the 1940s, but the diamond was under half a carat and a higher color, maybe an "I." Not worth what old Mr. Smith was asking for it, regardless of one's affinity for the forties.

When nothing in the vintage case sparked any interest in Fallon, they made their way case by case until they hit the one filled with Jack Smith's own creations. Most of the diamond engagement rings were under a carat—nothing too obvious to draw attention. Max thought Smith had probably hidden anything that might raise a brow after Summer O'Hara called out the Flower of Scotland. He had to give it to the old fox though, his designs were lovely. Some delicate and floral. Some more bold with mixtures of 18K yellow gold, rose gold, and platinum. All had high quality diamonds.

Fallon tried on three of the engagement rings, feigning interest in all of them. The shop was small, maybe 800 square feet. It didn't take long to exhaust the diamond selection. Then they moved to the small room housing sapphires, rubies, a few emeralds, multi-hued tourmalines, a handful of morganites, aquamarines, tanzanites, exactly three highly saturated amethyst rings, and a surprising selection of opals.

Max knew Fallon was feigning interest in the diamonds as soon as her eyes lit on the opals. They seemed to light a fire in her heart. For some reason that thrilled Max. Opals, especially ones from Australian mines that had run their course, could be every bit as expensive and far rarer than the white diamonds.

Seeing her interest, Max asked to see a strand of perfectly round opal beads.

Jack pulled them from the case, laying them out on a cushioned pad topped with black velvet. Then he grabbed the box they came in and set the box beside the stand. They were old, judging by the length, made for a small woman.

"These are from Vincent and Sons," Jack Smith said.

Max could have read that himself. It was written clearly in black script on the satin inside the cover of the hinged kidney bean shaped box.

"Vincent and Sons was a short-lived yet premier jeweler in Milwaukee at the turn of the last century. This piece dates back to the early 1900s, probably no later than 1920. The clasp is platinum, set with old mine cut diamonds." Jack held the strand up to the light filtering in from the front windows. There was plenty of incandescent light in the small space, but in the natural light, the green and blue hues of the opals appeared otherworldly. The piece was magnificent. Fit for someone who would love it as much as its creator had cared for its first recipient. Women just didn't wear things that rare and subtle today. Again, it pleased him that this piece was the one that brought a genuine smile to Fallon's face.

"Would you like to try it on?" Jack asked, obviously pleased to take out a piece of value that most people would simply ignore.

Fallon's hand went to her throat. "I…"

She caught herself quickly and started again. "It looks so delicate. I'm not sure I feel comfortable wearing it."

"I restrung these myself. I assure you, they are quite secure. You could wear this choker every day for the next decade, and as long as you took care not to swim in it, spray it full of perfume or hairspray, you'd have no issues."

Fallon tried it on. It fit perfectly.

"The total length is only fifteen and a half inches. Not everyone can wear this beauty."

Fallon looked at her reflection in the mirror. She looked like a princess. Her small smile and the look in her eyes as she stroked the beads made Max want to be the one who gave them to her. He wanted her to look at him while she touched him that reverently. He didn't dare entertain those kinds of thoughts. Not on the job. Not with Fallon. Not ever.

Before Max could direct Fallon's attention back to his real reason for being in the shop, she had the necklace off and was handing it to Jack Smith. "Thank you," she told him, meaning it, before she moved onto the next case.

Max made his way to a case that held pins made of sterling silver, replica coins taken from various ship wrecks, including some from the Atocha find. All were replicas. All were well done. None of them interested Max, because none housed any stolen gems he had on his radar.

Then Fallon, who was in the corner looking at sterling pendants, asked to see one of them. Max swung around to see what she found. She held it up for him. "Look, Max, it's a sterling impression of an old ring seal. The seal would have been used to imprint melted sealing wax to letters or other correspondence. Isn't it cool?"

Max went to her side. It was very cool indeed. Inside the seal was a tiny red diamond. No more than fifteen or sixteen points. Not the kind of thing to be placed in a pendant selling for just over a hundred bucks.

Max took the pendant and put it over Fallon's head. He turned to Jack Smith and said "Sold" as enthusiastically as he could. He didn't bother to hide his smile. "Now, my sweet girl, shall we pick out a diamond?"

Fallon grinned at him, went to the case where she'd seen the three wedding sets she liked, and pointed to the one that Max thought had the highest quality diamond. She picked a smallish diamond, over half a carat, but not quite sixty points, surrounded by a halo of small round diamonds with even smaller diamonds running down the shank. Most white diamonds under a carat didn't come with GIA—Gemological Institute of America certifications. This one didn't, but it was easy to see it was well cut and clearly in the white scale of D, E, or F color.

"We'll take the lady's choice," Max said to Jack.

Jack pulled out the ring and handed it to Max.

Max slipped it onto Fallon's left finger, on top of the thin eternity band he'd placed there less than an hour before. It fit perfectly.

His eyes captured hers. Before he changed his mind, he leaned down and brushed her lips with his. As kisses went, it wasn't more than a brief hello, still it shook him to his core. "I'll call Tiffany in Chicago and have a bigger one made for you if you want."

Jack interrupted. "I'll be happy to make the same ring in a larger size for Mrs.— "

He let the silence hang, waiting for Max to jump in with his last name.

Max said instead, "Fallon kept her maiden name. No

Mrs., just Fallon Murphy."

Jack nodded. "I'll be happy to make another ring for you if you determine you'd like more substance on your finger, Ms. Murphy. Just tell me about the size and what you're looking for, and I'll get some stones in for you to look at."

Fallon smiled at him. "Thank you, Mr. Smith. I think I'll live with this ring for a while before I decide. Right now, it has all the *substance* I can handle."

Max reached into his back pocket, pulled out his wallet, and set his white card down on the counter. "We'll take the ring and the pendant; we may be back for the opals."

They wouldn't be. Max took one look at the price on the antique strand and knew he'd be skinned alive if the deputy director got wind of that kind of purchase. His white card was real—issued by invitation only with basically no limit. He even got points toward booking private jet flights. Even so, the FBI would not be amused when the bill came through.

The card served its purpose though.

It gave Jack Smith Max's assumed name. The name, when checked, would show that he earned millions of dollars a year—more specifically, that he charged and payed off more than a quarter of a million dollars in the previous twelve months. He was a mover, a shaker, a man willing to spend fortunes large and small on the finer things in life, including jewelry.

For any criminal worth his or her salt, it also told them where Max Smart lived, worked, traveled, ate, drank, and that he was willing to part with his cash freely and frequently.

Jack Smith was worth his salt.

Max had just made himself a mark.

Now all they had to do was see if he was a big enough mark to tempt a thief who made his living ensuring he never got caught.

Either way, Max was determined to catch his white whale. The only difference was Max wouldn't let the whale take him down with him.

CHAPTER SIX

Walking into her mother's house knowing Summer wasn't there felt odd. The scents were the same. On a table near the door, lilacs and peonies sprouted from the tin-can vase Fallon had made for her mother in fourth grade. Another vase, an Irish crystal, was filled with Asian lilies and hybrid tea roses from Summer's garden in the back. Petals were falling from the lilies, but the roses still had their bloom. They seemed to scent the air even more strongly when they were in the last vestiges of life.

Fallon's stomach turned. Broken shards of Summer's tea cup, jagged and raw, the largest piece stained on the edge a sickening brown-red, lay scattered at the bottom of the stairs. Fallon had her hand to her mouth trying to control the wave of nausea when Max came up behind her and enveloped her in a hug. She turned into him and let him hold her.

One hand was at the small of her back, the other at her nape, holding her to him as he whispered, "It wasn't as bad as it looks. She had a small cut on her arm from the teacup." Actually, it was a gash that bled more than it should have. The doctor had said the compounds in the poison had thinned Summer's blood, making her bleed more profusely. The cut required about twenty stitches, but Fallon didn't need to hear that.

Max hoped that when they Skyped, Fallon wouldn't see Summer's bandages. "She bruised her arms and her left wrist. She's pretty banged up but nothing is broken. She's going to be all right."

Fallon pulled away from Max to look into his eyes. She wasn't crying exactly, but her eyes were red and glistening with unshed tears. "How do you know she's going to be all right? Someone tried to kill her."

"Because you and I, with a little help from our friends, will make it so."

"I don't have any friends here," Fallon said dejectedly.

Max smiled down at her, moving a piece of her shoulder-length hair behind her ear. "I highly doubt that. I've got a feeling you make friends wherever you go."

Fallon said nothing to that.

She wiped at her eyes with the back of her hand, taking what was left of her eye makeup and spreading it around. She had brownish sparkles around her temples and under her eyes. Nothing so mundane could take away from her earthy beauty. Fallon's features where strong, where her mothers were soft. She got her mother's spunk and apparently, her father's chiseled features. Gus had the same strong features. Max hadn't met Finn yet, but he was guessing Finn got the same chin, jaw, and cheekbones.

Fallon pushed away from him and bent to pick up the

shards of the broken teacup. "Thoughtless ass," she muttered to herself. "Bloody cretin couldn't be bothered to clean this up."

Max grabbed her by the arm, lifting her as gently as he could to her feet. "Give me those," he said opening his palm.

Fallon dropped the shards into his palm.

"I'll finish this. Why don't you go upstairs? Wash your face, comb your hair, do whatever you have to do to gear up for your brothers. As I understand it, you're the peacemaker of the group. Fingal is bound to be as furious as you are at Fergus. It's none of my business how your sibling dynamic works, but for what it's worth, Gus was trying to do what was right for your mom."

He had her for a moment. He lost her with his defense of Gus Murphy. Whatever was between them, whatever happened to Summer wasn't the beginning or end of it. The coldness in her eyes said Max had overstepped. Her words confirmed it.

"You're right. My siblings are none of your business." Her tone was flat when she said it. She was up the stairs and out of sight before Max could think of anything to say to bring some happiness back into her eyes.

"Way to go, Max. Alienate the one person you need to successfully complete your investigation," he muttered to himself. Muttering seemed to be contagious. Either that, or being married, even for show, was making him crazy.

By the time Max finished cleaning up the mess at the bottom of the stairs, taking out what was now rancid trash, and throwing away the dying flowers, he was starving.

There were no steaks in the refrigerator. He hadn't purchased any. He hadn't planned on having to stop Gus from doing whatever that hothead planned to do to Jack Smith. He hadn't planned how he was going to deal with the Murphy triplets at all.

Max found the keys to Summer's Mazda right where she told them they'd be. He penned a hasty note letting Fallon know where he was going, if she cared. He wrote it on a pad of paper secured by a magnet on the refrigerator that read "Things To Do" in bold block letters at the top and "Make the World Better with Your Smile" at the bottom.

He wasn't smiling when he walked out the front door.

So much for making the world a better place.

...

Jake Smith picked up one of his many burner phones and called the woman with the long blond hair. In reality, her hair was neither long nor blond. He knew her intimately. She did have certain attributes that made his life more lucrative, which made it far more palatable. And those side benefits suited him. For now.

She didn't answer.

Jack Smith left a message.

"I need you up here. Time for a ten-day vacation. Bring your toys."

The Fallon Murphy encounter made every hair on the back of Jack's neck stand at attention. It wasn't Fallon he needed to worry about. The man with her, the one claiming to be her husband, he was a threat. Jack thought he'd seen the man before, but he'd run his picture—taken from Jack's in-store surveillance—by every secure source he had. So far, he'd come up with nothing. The guy was smart. Knew how to avoid camera angles.

Time to get some surveillance in Summer O'Hara's house.

The funeral service tomorrow should be the perfect time to see it done. Most of the town would be at the service.

Jack Smith thought about the money still to be made from the stones he'd taken out of the stolen Zoe Tiara. He thought about all the money he had stashed around the world. He thought about his small cottage in the Cotswolds of England and the widowed teacher who lived next door. He thought about his apartment in Rome with a view of the Vatican.

Then he thought of his home in Long Grove, Illinois, and his summer home on the lake in Fish Creek, just south of his shop in Ephraim.

He was older than he ever thought he'd live to be. He was physically healthy and agile for his age. Even so, he couldn't scale walls with the same alacrity anymore. He didn't have the stamina. His reflexes had slowed, no matter how many exercises he did daily to keep them sharp. His upper body strength had waned, and sex was no longer a spontaneous thing, but a planned one, made possible with the help of pharmaceuticals.

Jack Smith really liked the widow in the Cotswolds. Liked the slow life there too. Flowers in the summer with evenings at the pub. Winters spent by the fire, reading, talking to the widow about books. Maybe even kissing her goodnight in time. It was appealing.

Jack put the thought away.

He was done running.

He liked his life here. He was going to live it as long as possible. Even if that meant cutting other lives short.

CHAPTER SEVEN

Fallon showered, changed into a pair of shorts and a T-shirt she had in her room. She kept a collection of clothing at her mother's house since she spent time here every summer. She also had clothing in the trunk of her rental that she packed in Key West. She just hadn't bothered to unpack yet.

Max was gone when she went downstairs. So were the wilted flowers. Fallon was thankful for that. She didn't like to see once beautiful living things fade into nothingness. She wasn't sure why she was feeling so morbid.

Then she looked at the ugly urn her brothers had picked for what at least Finn thought were their mother's ashes and she started to laugh. She laughed so hard it hurt. No wonder she was feeling morbid. She'd been carrying around some poor sod's ashes wishing she'd have called her mother more often.

Fallon made her way to the kitchen. She was hungry now that she didn't want to throw up. And she wanted to talk to her mother. The latter wouldn't happen until her brothers got here. A mixed blessing that. The former she could do something about.

The note on the frig stopped her in her tracks.

Hungry after our first argument. Gone out for grill food. Looking forward to make-up marital sex after we eat.

"Keep dreaming, Romeo," Fallon said smiling as she shook her head. She'd felt badly about snapping at him. It wasn't Max's fault she still felt raw about Gus's betrayal.

"Always keep the dream alive," Max said behind her.

Fallon whirled around, catching sight of him in his rumpled polo, khaki shorts, and ill-fitting boat shoes. It was the smile on his face and the devilish twinkle in his eye that made him dangerously appealing.

Fallon smiled back. "Never going to happen, slick."

He came closer to her, walking slowly, smiling so wickedly that her heart literally skipped a beat before racing in her chest. Then he leaned down, set the groceries on the counter behind her, and whispered, "Never is a long time, sweetheart. I wouldn't hold your breath."

Fallon turned toward him. Max held his breath, waiting to hear what she had to say. He'd been frustrated, mostly with himself, but somewhat with her, when he wrote that note. He didn't regret it, exactly. How could he when she looked freshly scrubbed and sweet and she was smiling at him like he was her best friend in the world.

That made something inside him explode.

Whatever else happened, Max was going to keep the woman next to him safe.

She was gearing up to give him a royal dressing down when a voice cut in. "So, it's true. You went and got married."

Max looked toward the entrance to the kitchen. A man who looked like Gus, except for the smile, stood with open arms, looking at Fallon with love in his eyes.

Fallon ran to him.

Finn spun her around like she was five and they were on the playground. "How could you let another man hold your heart without letting me and Gus give you away. That's always been the plan, short-stuff."

Since Fallon was almost as tall as her brothers, that comment was laughable on its face. They were all tall, dark, and attractive. Suddenly Max felt like a third wheel.

Then Gus walked in and he became the fourth wheel.

He was about to catch them up on the fact that he and Fallon weren't really married. He needed to do that before they talked to their mother. Fallon had other ideas. "Put me down, you oaf. I'm not a child anymore."

Finn set her down. "Nope. All grown up and frick'n *married*. What are you going to tell us next?" he asked feigning irritation, "that there's a tribe of mini-me's running around Key West?"

Fallon hit him. "Don't say *frick'n*. It makes you sound like an eleven-year-old afraid to swear for real." Then she grinned at him, ignoring Gus completely. "Come meet Max."

Fallon walked Finn toward him. She stopped about a foot away and introduced the brother he'd only seen in photos. "Max this is my brother Fingal. Finn, meet my...*husband*, Max Smart, business consultant extraordinaire."

Max just stared at her, eyes narrowed, silently asking what was going on.

Fallon winked at him.

Finn grabbed Max in a bear hug that threatened his ribs. Then he made it worse by pounding his back like he thought Max was choking to death. Finally, he let him go. Then pulled him in for another quick hug. Mercifully, this one was quick and not nearly so tight.

"Welcome to the family, Max," Finn said, still smiling. "You must be really something to get Fallon to marry you without telling her family."

"She's still pissed at me, Finn. That's probably why she didn't tell us," Gus said. His voice sullen, flat, angry. He was leaning against the wall that opened to the kitchen. The invisible chip on his shoulder weighing down his left side.

Again, Fallon ignored Gus. Max decided to do the same.

Finn lost his smile. His shoulders dropped and his chin dipped toward Fallon. "Did Mom know?" he asked. "She'd have been so happy for you, half-pint."

Fallon reached up and touched Finn's cheek. "No," she said. "Mom didn't know." Fallon shot Max a look that he thought meant, *don't say anything about us* not *being married.* That was okay with him. He liked having an excuse to hold her hand anytime he wanted. He had no problem with that.

Gus pushed away from the wall, looked at his watch, strode into the kitchen and said, "Isn't it time to get mom on the phone?"

Finn whirled around to face Gus, hands fisted at his sides. "That was a terrible joke."

Gus put his hands behind his back. "No joke." His gaze went to Max. "Call her."

Finn looked from Fallon to Gus then back at Fallon.

"I just found out. Still don't quite believe it," she said.

Finn turned to Gus. "How long have you known?"

"Since the beginning. Since Max saved her," Gus said. No excuses. No empathy for what either of his siblings had been put through because he'd lied to them.

Finn punched him in the face.

For the second time in a matter of hours, Max was cleaning blood off the floor.

CHAPTER EIGHT

The journey to Milwaukee had been uneventful, which according to Rolly made it perfect. It took them two days to get there, a short time by most standards. For Summer, it was too long to be stuck on a boat. When Rolly was playing cards with her, she was fine. When he was rubbing her ankles, she was fine—better than fine, but she didn't need to tell him that.

Summer wasn't fine when she was alone while Rolly was doing what needed to done to keep them on the right course. She tried not to show it, but somehow Rolly knew. He wasn't patronizing about it; he didn't tell her how brave she was. What he did do was read to her. He played cards with her. He never let her win, which she did about forty percent of the time. The man was a cardsharp. He bluffed like a man born to it.

His condo surprised her. It overlooked the river and had a slip where Rolly docked his boat. The view was spectacular. It was in an area of the city referred to as the Third Ward—a closed art community with boutique shops and some of the city's best restaurants. The condo itself was bright and cheery, done in a shade of grey and cream and burgundy. The kitchen was outfitted for a man who loved to cook. There were two bedrooms, both en suite. One she currently lived in. The other, she hadn't seen. There was a large and open great-room that led to the balcony, which was large enough to hold a grill, a bistro set, and two full-length reclining loungers.

The art on the wall was local. Her favorites were the lithographs done by Wisconsin artist Harold Hansen. Rolly had a large loom against the wall. The man loomed in his spare time which, as far as Summer could tell, he didn't have much of. Rolly was constantly in motion. Up early. Go all day. To bed by eleven, generally after some snuggle time on the couch watching movies.

Rolly liked action movies, old Hitchcock flicks, and the remake of *Westworld*.

She liked *Midsomer Murders*, *NCIS*, and everything with Pierce Brosnan—including *Mama Mia* which Rolly watched with one arm around a gigantic bowl of cheese popcorn, the other around her.

As lovely as his home was, Summer was going more than a little stir-crazy. She also wanted to see another human being, even if she wasn't allowed to talk to them.

Summer was sitting in the kitchen drinking her third cup of coffee—something Rolly said wasn't good for her—when he walked in, hair still wet from his shower. He grabbed a mug from the mug tree and poured himself a cup from the pot. He leaned against the back counter, looking at her as she read the *Post* from his tablet. "Is that your third cup?"

Summer set down her cup and looked Rolly straight in the eye. He was wearing a pair of tan shorts, a white polo shirt, and grey running shoes. "This is my *second* cup of coffee, Rolly Scott. And for your information, I am a grown woman who can decide for herself how much caffeine she can ingest."

The corner of his mouth twitched, but he didn't smile. "Liar."

Summer didn't even try to fight it. "How do you always know?"

Rolly crossed the room and sat on the stool beside her. "You always look me in the eye and use my full name. Then you get defensive and say something like, 'Rolly, I am perfectly capable of making my own poor decisions.'" Rolly mimicked her voice, but he got the pitch too high and cadence too slow. Even so, he was pretty good.

"I don't make poor decisions." Summer shrugged. Letting Jack Smith know she knew he had the Flower of Scotland had been a doozie. She flushed. "Not most of the time anyway. And certainly not about coffee."

Rolly changed the subject, which Summer was beginning to learn signaled he was certain he was right and thought he'd made his point well enough to move on.

"I've got a surprise for you," he said.

"Do I get to finish my coffee?"

He grinned at her, then leaned down and kissed the top of her head. Summer couldn't tell who was more surprised, him or her, but he didn't stop grinning at her. He seemed quite pleased with himself. "Drink up, darlin'. I'll be right back."

Suddenly her coffee wasn't so necessary anymore. Summer was wide awake and having more fun than she'd had in years. What she wasn't, she realized, was lonely.

Rolly came back holding a box about a foot wide and a foot deep. It was white with a big red bow on top. Summer looked from the box to Rolly, then back at the box. "What's this?" she asked.

Rolly seemed almost giddy. He was certainly pleased with himself. "Open it. Find out."

He handed the box to Summer.

She lifted the top. She couldn't quite believe her eyes. "Are we role playing?"

Rolly spit out the coffee he'd been trying to swallow.

Summer lifted a wig out of the box. It was blond and cut short. She put it on. "Is this a gentlemen-prefer-blondes thing?"

"No. And for the record, this gentleman prefers redheads. This," he said nodding toward the wig, "is a let's-get-out of-the-condo-and-enjoy-ourselves thing. There's a pair of sunglasses in there too. I'd like you to wear a hat. I've got an extra Brewers cap that should fit."

"We can get out of here?"

"That's the plan."

Summer squealed, jumped up, threw her arms around Rolly, then ran toward her bathroom at the opposite end of the hall. When Rolly bought the condo, having the two master bedrooms on opposite ends had been a selling point. Now that he actually had a house guest, *this* house guest, he wanted her right next him. He was falling for

Summer O'Hara. A woman he was supposed to be protecting. A woman who had two good marriages and by all accounts loved two good men.

He was two-time loser. He loved one great woman, he cared about two pretty good ones, and he managed to lose all three. One by a quirk of fate no one could control. Two by being a distant, self-important ass. Fate had nothing to do with that.

Now fate, or God, or the Universe had entrusted him with caring for another great woman. One who was nothing like his first love, except in her inherent kindness. One who made him laugh, kept him questioning his opinions, who couldn't lie worth a damn, and seemed to find the positive in the least positive of situations. This woman made his heart beat faster while still being so easy to be around he didn't have to try. This woman was the whole package. The thought of losing Summer scared him like he hadn't been scared since the day they got Peggy's diagnosis.

Summer came out of her room wearing her wig. It worked. She looked different enough that no one who didn't scrutinize her closely would know she was Summer O'Hara. Rolly wouldn't let anyone within scrutinizing range of Summer, so he could show her a good time in his city without worry. He was happy he could do this for her. That he'd enjoy her enjoyment was an added bonus.

She twirled for him.

Rolly loved the fact that Summer didn't act like she was older than she was. She enjoyed life and she let it show. "How do I look?"

The wig was shorter than her shoulder-length hair. She looked younger with the bangs, but that could have been the ear-to-ear grin. "Like Kelly Preston when she was blond."

Summer laughed. "Now who's lying, Rolly Scott?"

He wasn't lying, although Summer was more attractive than Kelly Preston and less flashy. "Come on, woman. Let's get out of here."

Summer was at the door, purse slung across her body, sunglasses in hand before he could fish the keys out of his pocket.

For the first time in a long time, Rolly was looking forward to simply spending the day out with a woman.

...

"So, tell me about your son," Summer said, popping a strawberry in her mouth. Rolly took her to breakfast at a sidewalk café that specialized in fruit crepes. She had a double order. One strawberry. One blueberry. Both were fantastic.

Rolly set down his fork. He'd finished about half his spinach omelet and red potato hash. "I thought we weren't talking about our kids."

"Five minutes."

"Okay. What do you want to know?" Rolly asked.

"What kind of man is he?"

The question threw Rolly for a second. Most people asked for the mundane facts: Where does he work? Is he married? Do you see each other often? Not Summer. But then she wasn't most people.

What kind of man was Max? Rolly said the first word that came to his mind, "Honorable."

Summer's eyebrows raised and she pulled down her sunglasses far enough to look over the rims at him. "That's it?"

Rolly narrowed his eyes. "Is there anything I could say about Max right now that would mean more to you than that?"

Summer thought about it for a second, and just when Rolly thought she'd ask him something more, she said, "No. Thank you."

Again, she surprised him. This time pleasantly. He was sinking deeper under her spell and he didn't care. "Tell me about your children," Rolly said, although the one he cared about most was Fallon. Fallon had his son's attention.

"Gus came out first. He was plucked, actually. Ever since then, he thinks it's his job to run the show, whatever the show is. He's smart, ambitious, and hard-headed. He has a good heart, and he tries to do the right thing but manages to put his foot in it about a third of the time."

Summer ate another strawberry, warming to her topic. "Fingal is kind, and funny, and determined. He makes everything work. His focus is amazing. He has a tender heart that gets him in trouble more than it should. That hasn't made him jaded though. He still puts himself out there with more optimism than I could muster."

Rolly said nothing, but he doubted that. He'd never met another person as openly optimistic as Summer. He was betting Fingal Murphy had a sizable amount of his mother in him.

Rolly took a sip of his water, urging Summer to continue with a gesture.

She smiled, though not at him. She was staring off, lost in a memory, and judging by her expression, it was a fond one. "Fallon is a mix of both boys and," Summer paused, "she's all her own. She opens her heart, but not with regularity or blind optimism. She's strong and opinionated. That manifests as stubbornness and determination, depending on how the recipient of her strength takes it. Fallon loves hard. And when she cares deeply, she gives everything she's got to the person or project she cares about. She's loyal and seriously smart. She's got a good head for business." Summer looked right at him. "And if she feels she's been wronged, she's slow to forgive." She paused again just to make sure he understood what she was saying. "My girl holds a grudge."

Rolly got the distinct impression that Summer wasn't simply talking about her daughter.

"You're not going to scare me off, Summer. No matter how hard you try. I can out stubborn the best of them. And you, my dear, are not in the running for stubborn blonde of the year. I don't think Max is going to do anything that would give Fallon a reason to hold a grudge."

Rolly smiled at her and leaned in. "It's not like he married her, moved in, and set up house. There should be no legitimate reason for Fallon to hold a grudge."

For some reason Rolly couldn't define, Summer's slow smile bothered him. It reminded him again that women were inherently undefinable and infinitely more complex than their male counterparts. That even when they appear simple and sweet and straightforward, they almost always know more than you do.

Summer lifted her glass of iced tea in salute. "Of course, you're right," she said, solidifying his concern. "What on earth would lead any of my children to hold a grudge against Max. He did save my life after all."

Rolly groaned inwardly knowing he was going to get more than he bargained with Summer, yet grateful she was such a bad liar. One thing he knew for absolute certain, out of everything she'd just said, Summer O'Hara only believed her last sentence.

Rolly got up, slid two twenty-dollar bills into the over-sized black wallet that contained their bill, and reached for Summer. "Come on then, lovely lady. It's a beautiful day and we've got a lot to do before the sky opens up and your proverbial *grudge shoe* drops on our heads."

Summer grinned at him. "Our children's five minutes are up, sir," she said standing before executing a sloppy but endearing bow. "The rest of the day is all ours."

Now that kind of thinking, Rolly thought, was more like it.

CHAPTER NINE

All three of the Murphy children stared at Max's laptop screen, trying to decipher the surreal experience of speaking to a mother they were having difficulty recognizing. Each one was lost in their own internal space: Gus, biting down hard on the peanuts he kept popping into his mouth; Fingal, silently assessing, lips pursed, head cocked to one side; Fallon, openly engaged in disbelief.

For his part, Max was having a hard time reconciling his reserved, by-the-book father with the smiling, seemingly happy-go-lucky man on the screen sitting next to a now blond Summer O'Hara.

"After breakfast, Rolly took me to something called the Rainbow Race where rainbow-colored chalk is thrown on the racers as they run by. They end up being a mess, but everyone seems to enjoy it."

"It's not chalk. It's called the Color Run," Rolly interjected.

Summer waived that away, then took Rolly's hand when he tried to adjust the screen on his laptop and held it.

"That's not really important, is it?" she asked.

Rolly smiled indulgently at her. "Nope."

"What's important is that we had *such* a great time today," Summer said expansively, gesturing at the screen with her free hand. Then she leaned in and said conspiratorially, "Did you know there's a place called The Witches House on the lake? Not only is it haunted by a real witch who never dies, she's an artist and her lawn is filled with exotic sculptures."

"Mom, what's that on your head?" Fallon asked.

"It's a wig, dear." Summer whispered, "I'm incognito. Isn't it exciting?"

Max started to cough.

Finn said, "I think she's asking about the headband with the springs on it."

Summer's hand flew to her head. Then she looked at Rolly with a frown. "Why didn't you tell me I still had this thing on?"

Rolly laughed. A sound Max hadn't heard from his father in more than a year. "It's cute."

"What *is* it?" Finn asked, sounding truly curious and far less judgmental than his brother looked.

"Rolly bought this," she said seriously, peering into the screen. "It has tiny bouncing rainbows attached to it." Summer nodded as if her explanation made perfect sense.

Rolly added, "After lunch we walked to the Summerfest grounds. I took your mother to Pride Fest. That," he said nodding toward the bouncing rainbows on Summer's head, "was the least flamboyant thing she liked. It looked cute on her when she tried it on, so I bought it for her."

"Were the heart-shaped glasses your idea too?" Max asked, thinking his father had lost his mind.

"Nope. I got her a nice pair of Oakley's. She picked up the ones she's wearing from a vender on the Summerfest grounds for five bucks."

"Best deal of the day." Summer nodded, making the tiny rainbows bounce.

Fallon was shaking her head, a perplexed look on her face. It's not even seven thirty yet, Mom. Just how much wine have you had?"

Summer smiled and lifted her plastic cocktail glass. "We're sitting on the balcony watching the river. Rolly made mojitos." She took a sip from her glass. "They're delicious."

Finn smiled at his mother. "How many have you had, Mom?"

"This is my second," Summer said, holding up an almost full glass.

"Third," Rolly interjected.

Summer let go of his hand and back-handed him gently across the chest. "Noooo," she said. "This is like that coffee thing, right? I've only had two, but you count three." Summer looked from Rolly back toward the screen. "Rolly doesn't want me to drink more than two cups of coffee." She sounded put out by that.

Gus spoke around a handful of nuts for the first time. "But apparently three mojitos *are* okay."

Everyone ignored him.

Finn grinned. He looked like he was enjoying himself. He'd only just learned that his mother was alive. After punching his brother and seeing his mother on the screen, he seemed to be over the hurt and fully embracing the joy of seeing his mother happy. Or that's how it appeared to Max. Finn was pretty easy to figure out. He was having a harder time reading what Fallon was thinking.

Finn grabbed Fallon's left hand and held it up to the screen, grinning. "Since you're in the mood to celebrate, here's some good news." He waved Fallon's hand, holding it firm as she tried to pull it away, "Fallon's married."

Max waited for the explosion he thought was imminent. If not from Summer, then from his father.

Both parents looked at the screen, taking in the sight of Fallon's left hand and the diamond rings resting there.

A slow smile began to move across Summer's face. She looked at Rolly as if their children on the screen were no longer part of the conversation. "I think, Sir Rolly, that the sky just opened. You better watch out so that *grudge shoe* doesn't fall on your head."

Rolly smiled at Summer. Then all four children watched in amazement as he took off Summer's wig, taking the bouncing headband with it. Then he kissed her. "My head will be just fine, darling. So, will yours, after tomorrow."

Rolly looked back at the screen, his gaze finding Max. "I hope you know what you're doing," he said. Then he looked back at Summer. "Say good night to your children, sweetheart. They seem to need assurance that you're okay."

Summer looked at the screen. "I'm more than okay. I'm enjoying myself immensely. Take care, loves," she said.

Then Rolly closed the computer, leaving them all to wonder how a woman who was supposed to be dead wound up enjoying life like a giddy teenager.

. . .

Seeing the look on Fallon's face, or more accurately, judging the air around her, Max asked her brothers to leave. "We all have a big day tomorrow," he said, referring to Summer's memorial service. "We should all get some sleep."

Finn kissed his sister's cheek on his way out saying, "Doesn't it feel good not to have secrets?"

Fallon pushed him out the door. "Mom should have named you, Loki. The trickster role suits you."

Gus left without a kiss or so much as a wave and a "see you tomorrow."

That was fine with Max. Tolerating Gus was beginning to feel like a full-time job.

Fallon shut the front door and surprised Max by saying, "It's still light out. Want to take a walk down by the water?"

Max wasn't sure why Summer wanted to get out of the house. Maybe it was as simple as wanting some fresh air. It had been one heck of a day for her. Not wanting to read anymore into it than that, he said, "Sure. Let me just change my shoes." He smiled. "I've been told the ones I'm wearing don't suit me."

Max ran upstairs to the room he'd staked out as his, rummaged through his duffle, and grabbed his running shoes. He quickly put them on. Then he went to his second secure computer and pulled up the security feed from the cameras and other monitoring devises he'd had installed immediately after his covert op was authorized. By the time Summer's fake death certificate had been penned, her entire property had been rigged with monitoring devises, some of which were geared to alert Max of any intrusion through his cell phone.

None of the alarms had been triggered. No unscheduled activity around the house—although there was footage of Fallon cutting fresh flowers from her mother's garden. Even in black and white, she was beautiful.

Max closed his computer, locked it in the high-density plastic box he kept it in, and placed the box in his duffle, right next to his backup weapon. He kicked the duffle under the bed. Not much of a hiding spot, but for now it would do.

He ran downstairs to meet his *wife*.

CHAPTER TEN

While Max was busy upstairs, Fallon texted her boss, Nick Card, asking what he'd discovered about stolen jewels entering the private collections via the gray and black markets. Fallon didn't know all Nick's connections, probably not even ten percent of them. The one's she knew were sufficient for her to know whatever Nick told her was the absolute truth.

He texted back: *Sending a friend to check on you.*

That wasn't good. That meant Nick was significantly worried about her safety, even knowing she had her own personal FBI agent at her side—more than anyone else had been in months.

How bad is it? Fallon texted.

Her phone rang a second later.

Nick's resonant voice sounded in her ear before she could say hello. "I've verified that several stones have made their way from Chicago to Miami and from there to London, Mumbai, Zurich, Rome, and Berlin. Three of the stones have been authenticated as coming from the Zoe

Tiara. The Flower of Scotland is still unaccounted for. Given its provenance and the lore behind the theft, whoever stole it has a fluid and active market for gems— something worth killing for. Whoever purchased it has a vested interest in keeping it. That makes them dangerous too. Maybe more so."

"So, you're telling me to watch my back," Fallon said.

"I'm telling you I'm sending someone to watch your back. I need you to finish your business up there and come back. I need you back here. Having you near me dissuades the casual criminals from any number of bad acts."

Fallon snorted. "And it encourages the diehards."

"True enough." Nick paused and grew even more serious. "I've run a check on this FBI agent, quietly. He's smart. Overly ambitious when it comes to catching those involved in the spate of thefts that involved the stones your mother identified. He's honest, like his father before him, but reckless. Where his father lived by the rules, your man plays a bit fast and loose. Normally I'd cast that as an asset, but not this time. Not with you. Take care, love."

"Always," Fallon said.

"I've got a feeling things will be coming to a head there. That photo of the small stone you texted looks like one of nineteen other red diamonds from the Zoe Tiara. The one you just bought from Jack Smith for $120 is one of the smaller stones. Given its provenance, it would fetch over $100,000 on the gray market."

"Jack Smith doesn't know we know we bought a red diamond and not a garnet or a piece of polished glass."

"Don't bet on it, love. He let you walk out of his store

with it because he could kill you in his shop. He won't take any chances. That stone—hiding in plain sight—is proof he possessed stolen gems. No way he can explain that away easily. Even if there's not enough proof to indict him, INTERPOL and the FBI will be watching him every day for the rest of his life. He'll be audited. He'll be hounded. He'll never lead a normal life again."

"Does he know my mom's alive?"

Nick Card took a deep breath. "No. For now your mother is safe. It's you I'm worried about."

"I can take care of myself."

Nick sighed audibly into the phone. "Where's the necklace with the red diamond now?"

Fallon's hand went to the chain around her throat. She ran her fingers over the pendant, wondering how such a small stone could cause so many people to lose their minds. "I'm wearing it."

"Are you in the house?"

"Yes."

"When you click off, I want you to go outside. Walk the length of the patio that faces Jack Smith's store. Make sure you have the necklace visible. Play with it as you look at your mother's flowers. Then go in the house. Are the blinds open on the windows in your mother's kitchen?"

Fallon looked. "Yes."

"Good. Take the necklace off. Leave it in that crystal bowl your mother keeps on the kitchen table."

Nick had been to her mother's house exactly once. It was so like Nick to remember every detail—especially the layout of the rooms and every access point. Nick Card was a thief at heart, albeit a good-hearted one.

"You should add your watch to the bowl and your earrings if you're wearing them," Nick added.

"It's not like Jack Smith is watching my every move, Nick."

Fallon could hear the smile in Nick's voice. Her mentor had bone-deep affection for her. "I find your naiveté endearing most of the time. This time, dear heart, it's getting in the way. Do as I say. Leave the necklace. Leave the house. With any luck, the necklace will be gone when you return. Whatever you do, don't check the dish until the morning. When you come back home, go straight upstairs."

His next words stopped her heart. "Do not sleep alone tonight. I love you," he said, ending the call.

Fallon put the phone in her pocket and went outside to wait for Max. She did exactly as Nick instructed. She toyed with the necklace burning its way into her flesh as she imagined herself being watched. She pulled a few stray pieces of grass that found their way into her mother's planting beds. Then she went back into the house and turned on the kitchen light. Even though the late evening sun was filtering through the windows, there was little direct light. The kitchen light brightened the room, making it glow warmly. She took off her watch, setting it in the crystal bowl. Then her earrings. Finally, the necklace with its blood red stone. She was about to grab a soda from the refrigerator when Max came bounding down the stairs.

"I'm ready for our walk," he said.

"Let's go." Fallon wondered how long she would be playing the role of wife and grieving daughter. To her surprise, Fallon didn't mind the first one. The grieving part she didn't like one bit. She fervently hoped when this was over, no one in her family would have reason to grieve for decades.

...

It was a lovely evening. The breeze was light enough not to be bothersome but strong enough to keep away the tiny flying bugs from the lake. They left the house just after eight. The sun wasn't due to set for another half an hour or so. It was Fallon's favorite time of the day.

People raved about the evenings in Key West. Key West sunsets were said to be some of the most beautiful in the world. They were. No doubt. But the sunsets over Lake Michigan from Egg Harbor, Fish Creek, Ephraim, or Sister Bay were just as beautiful. Having grown up in the Door, Fallon thought even more so, although she'd never tell Nick Card that. Nick liked to tease that a good part of the reason he spent as much time in Key West was because of the hypnotic sunsets.

"Want to go to Wilson's and get ice cream? We could take it down by the beach. Hang in the Adirondack chairs for a while?" Max asked.

Fallon looked at him in surprise. "How do you know about Wilson's?" Wilson's burger and ice cream shop had been the cornerstone business in Ephraim for well over a hundred years. The red-and-white candy-striped exterior dotted with old Coke signs was the subject of many Door County artists over the years. To say it was iconic for Door

County would be like saying the Statue of Liberty was iconic for the nation.

"Anyone who's ever been to Ephraim knows Wilson's," Max said, smiling at her. He seemed tuned up, ready for action, as if he was anticipating something but not quite ready to share what that something was. He was calm, but there was an energy about him, humming just under the surface.

"Have you been to Ephraim before?"

"Not in a long time. When I came up as a kid with my parents, we stayed in Egg Harbor. We'd camp sometimes in Peninsula State Park, but we rarely went farther north than Fish Creek." He smiled down at her, "But we made it to Wilson's once or twice."

Fallon wanted to ask more. She wanted to *know* more about Max as a child. That thought got waylaid when he asked about Gus.

"What is with two anyway?" he asked. "I get that he's a jerk, but your anger with him seems far deeper than that."

"It is."

"Do you want to talk about it?"

Fallon took Max's hand and led him to the small bench in front to the library just down from Wilson's. If they were going to talk about this, she wanted them to be alone—not surrounded by tourists eating burgers, enjoying fountain sodas, or devouring every kind of ice cream known to man.

Max sat next to Fallon on the bench, keeping her hand in his. She didn't pull away. His warmth and his presence were comforting.

Did she want to talk about it? Fallon thought about that

for a moment while they sat silently watching the world go by. She really liked Max's ability to cut through to what mattered, and that he was content to sit with her while she hashed it all out inside.

Without making the conscious decision to open up to Max, she just did. It was easy.

"I think commercial fishermen are a lot like cops and professional soldiers," she said.

That didn't make immediate sense to Max, but he didn't interrupt. He'd found that the best way to get to the truth was to let it come without interruption or leading. He'd have made a terrible lawyer, he mused, silently urging Fallon to continue. After collecting her thoughts, she did. Tied it all up rather nicely too, he thought.

"They worry. They know their profession is dangerous, so they leave notes or letters for their loved ones just in case heaven finds them before they're ready to go."

Max couldn't fault the logic of that. He had just that kind of letter addressed to his father.

"When we turned twenty-one, our mom gave us our letters from our father. Those were his instructions and Mom loved him enough to follow them."

Max couldn't imagine receiving one of those letters. It would be far worse than writing them, he thought. Now that his father was fully retired, he was fairly certain he'd never be in the position of finding out. Max rubbed the inside of Fallon's wrist with his thumb. She probably didn't realize it, but she was holding onto him tighter than before. Max wished then and there that if it were possible, he'd be granted the ability to take away at least some of her pain.

"All the letters were short. Dad telling each of us how much he loved us. How we made him smile. That he carried us in his heart every moment of every day. How he was the luckiest man in the world to be blessed with a wife who loved him and three babies who proved every day that heaven was a place he lived in on earth. That's how he put it. 'Every day was heaven, so long as he drew breath.'"

Fallon blinked away tears in her eyes and gave him a watery smile. "My father had an Irish poet's soul."

Max wanted to pull Fallon to him. He wanted to hold her for the rest of his life. He was betting Fingal and Fallon had their own poet's soul. The jury was still out on whether Fergus possessed a soul at all.

"With the letters were gifts. One for each of us." Fallon paused, swallowing hard. "Things that defined who our father was and what he cared about the most. Things even as children we'd seen and known he cared about."

Now Max wanted to prompt her. What could be so hurtful about a gift? It didn't make any sense to him. He trusted it would, but so far, the story didn't match Fallon's depth of emotion.

"To truly understand, you have to know that my father loved his parents and his grandparents deeply. He loved his grandfather most of all. Whenever he was on shore, he carried his grandfather's gold pocket watch. Always. Without fail. It was the single most important thing to him. He didn't love our house as much as he loved that watch."

"What were the other gifts?" Max asked, interjecting because Fallon looked like she was going to cry. He didn't want that if it could be helped. He wasn't good with crying females as a rule. The thought of Fallon crying damn near broke his heart. He thought he knew how this story was going to play out, but he was mistaken.

"My great-grandmother's engagement ring—a small ruby surrounded by tiny diamonds. She married the man with the watch."

"And…" Max prompted.

"And my father's rose-gold signet ring. His parents gave it to him as a graduation gift when he graduated from Trinity College in Dublin. He was so proud of that ring. He used to put it over my big toe and tell me if I studied very hard, I could have a ring like his someday."

Max smiled at her. The tears that threatened earlier were gone now, replaced by a watery, but warm smile. Max wanted to take Fallon to a place where he could see that grow, so he asked a question he hoped would take her there. "What did your father study at Trinity?"

She laughed, giving him a glimpse of her heart. "English. Dad didn't just have a poet's soul. He had a poet's mind as well."

Whether she realized it or not, Fallon had fallen into a native Irish cadence. A hold over from a childhood filled with Irish rhyme and rhythm, no doubt. He didn't have to prompt her this time to continue. She looked straight at him. No more misty-eyed dew, just sadness, reflected in her clear blue eyes.

"I got the pocket watch. Fingal got our great-grandmother's engagement ring. Gus got dad's signet ring." Fallon waited for him to understand. Max knew she was waiting because her expression said *Do you get it now?*

"I don't get it," Max said.

He didn't. He didn't get it at all.

Fallon took a deep breath in. She held it. Then she let it out again. She repeated that sequence three times before she tried to explain. Someone had taught her that. No one breathed with that kind of mindfulness without guidance.

"My mom had to have a C-section. The three of us were simply too big for her body." A statement of fact. Max got that. It was the rest of the connections that he was missing.

"Our birth order was chosen by the surgeon." She paused as if this bit of information was vital.

Max said nothing.

What could he say? Since nothing came to mind, he waited.

"Gus came first," Fallon said with the gravity Max imagined God had when giving the ten commandments to Moses.

"So?" Max asked.

Fallon jerked backward as if he'd slapped her. She gave an involuntary shake of her head. Then she seemed to realize she was speaking to someone who didn't give a flying-fig about triplet dynamics. She actually smiled. "So, Gus seems to think that because the surgeon chose to pull him from our mother first," Fallon gestured with her free hand jerking it rapidly in front of her, "And, because he was born with a penis, he was entitled to the gift he believed our father cared about most."

"Okay," Max said, trying to keep up. "So, your father told all three of you what gift he cared about most? He ranked them?"

This time Fallon scrunched her face up, threw her head back, and let out a sound that was both irritated and thankful. It sounded something like a duck gurgling. What Max heard was *urrrrggghhh*. What he saw on Fallon's face was a small, thankful smile. What he felt, he didn't care to contemplate. Who met their soulmate in a day? Certainly not a man old enough to know such things didn't exist.

"No! My father didn't rank his gifts in order of importance any more than he ranked his children."

That revelation seemed to stop Fallon in her tracks. She stopped talking. She stopped everything and just sat still for more seconds than Max could count. Then she laughed. It was the kind of laugh that said she'd just figured out something she should have realized long ago.

"No," she said. "Dad didn't rank us in his head or in his heart. He simply gave each of us what he thought we'd appreciate most. I think he also cared about which of us would pass the stories and the items on to our children and grandchildren. The *passing on* is important in my family," Fallon said as if Max didn't understand the concept. He got it. He had his own bits of memorabilia and his own stories to tell.

Now that Fallon wasn't about to cry, Max had to ask, "What's the big deal? I'm not obtuse. I'm just not following. What was your gift."

"Dad gave me his pocket watch." Fallon said it like she'd just put the nails in her own coffin.

"Okay…What did Gus get?"

"My father's signet ring—the ring marking his crowning

scholastic achievement," Fallon said. There wasn't much to add to that, so she continued with Finn's gift.

"Fingal got our great-grandmother's engagement ring," Fallon said.

"Was Finn happy?" Max asked.

"Thrilled," Fallon answered.

"Then why the angst?" Max said.

"Because Gus thought our father cared more about his pocket watch than anything else. He also thought he was the oldest, he was entitled to it. That it should have gone to him because he was the oldest son."

"That explains why Gus would be angry with you." Max shook his head. "Although that reasoning is full of holes when looked at logically." Max lifted Fallon's chin, trying to get her to focus on him and the fact that what she was saying was ridiculous on its face. "Why would you be angry about Gus's adolescent theatrics over a pocket watch verses a signet ring?"

Max regretting his words the second they left his mouth.

He never wanted to see the absence of emotion he saw in Fallon's eyes ever again. It cut him to the quick. When she spoke this time, she sounded like a robot. All emotion was gone. There was no love in her voice or her intonation.

There was no hate. Just no emotion at all.

In that moment, Max knew what hell looked like.

Hell wasn't pain.

It was apathy.

And it was written all over Fallon's face when she said, "I was never angry over the watch, or the ring, or Gus's manufactured hurt." She paused. Her expression grew even more distant—as if hell wasn't distant enough.

"Then why the disconnect?" Max asked.

"First, Gus saw something he thought was one thing, but wasn't."

"Well, that's clear as mud," Max said.

"He saw my college boyfriend kissing me goodbye. I had told him I'd just gotten engaged to my high school sweetheart. The man I thought I'd marry was Gus's best friend. Gus told him I was cheating on him with my college boyfriend. *That*," Fallon said, "caused my engagement to come to an abrupt end. That was right after Mom gave each of us our letters from dad. The day after our twenty-first birthday."

None of that was good. Still, it was forgivable, given time.

"Then…"

"Then?" Max asked, thinking he'd heard enough to punch Gus's lights out.

"Then, Gus took one look at me and said, 'Just wait until Mom dies.' He actually said those exact words. 'Just wait until mom dies.' I couldn't believe it at the time. I still can't quite believe it as I'm telling you this."

Fallon stopped talking.

It was as if her next words had been stolen from her. Like after all these years, she still couldn't make sense of Gus's nonsensical words. She seemed stymied.

Then she looked at him quizzically, like she was questioning her ability to think clearly. "Can you imagine anyone related to you being excited about the prospect of your mother's death?"

He couldn't. Max wanted to make Fallon a twin in that moment, but Fallon wasn't done with the hurt that Gus had reigned down upon her.

"Gus couldn't wait to try to punish me with it. He's twisted in a way I don't want to understand. I'm pretty sure I'll never forgive him for taking joy in the thought of our mother's death and how it might serve him as executor of her estate." Fallon paused. "I thought I'd gotten past all that. Then I learned he knew from the start Mom was alive. He kept that from me. He kept it from Finn too. Four days I've spent thinking our mother was dead." She looked at him sideways, "Can you imagine if those four days turned into three months?"

Max couldn't think of one excuse for Gus Murphy.

Fallon wasn't done. She was angry now and Max wanted her to revel in her anger. Fallon needed to call it out and move on. If he had his way, she'd be moving on without a brother. That man was toxic. No doubt about it. Max just wished he'd get a chance to make Fergus Murphy hurt for the pain he seemed to dish out like candy. God willing, he'd get that chance.

"My brother wanted to take every bit of my mother from me. He took her rings, the only jewelry I ever cared about, from me. Then he took pleasure in making me believe she was dead."

Fallon looked at him clearly and said, "I'll do almost anything to keep my mother safe. I'll do anything you ask me too. Just don't ask me to give Gus a pass. I'm simply not capable of that kind of grace."

"Screw Gus. He's a vitriolic waste of space and he isn't worth your time right now. We've got bigger things to worry about now, like keeping your mother and you safe."

Fallon agreed.

"Help me do that."

Fallon was listening.

"I need you to be my wife until this is over. I don't want to do anything to make you uncomfortable, but I need you to act like you love me."

Fallon held firm to Max's hand. "Okay," she said, meaning it.

CHAPTER ELEVEN

Max walked Fallon upstairs. He showed her the room he set up in, including all his equipment. She didn't need to go into the kitchen to determine that the sterling necklace with the red diamond was gone. It was on the screen, clear as day.

Only it wasn't Jack Smith who broke in to retrieve it. It was a woman. A woman with long blond hair and shaded glasses. Flashy. Elegant even. The kind of woman no one would mistake and everyone would remember.

Max put a finger to his lips, gesturing to Fallon that she should watch what she said. He went to his phone and texted her, while he said, "Should we snuggle and watch a movie? Take both our minds off the memorial service tomorrow?"

He texted: *That's the woman your mother took a cell phone photo of from Jack's store. She saw the woman with The Flower of Scotland and one time before that buying what we believe is a stolen Harry Winston diamond.*

Fallon nodded toward the phone. "Sure honey. That

sounds great. I'm not looking forward to tomorrow. I don't want to get up in front of all those people and say anything. I'll let Gus and Finn do that."

"You don't have to do anything you don't want to," Max said.

Fallon texted back: *Are they listening to us?*

Doubtful. Still, we should be cautious. Need to act like everything is as it appears to be. Mom dead. We're married. Nothing to see here.

Got it, Fallon typed.

And she did get it. What she didn't get was her reaction. She was comfortable around him. She didn't mind letting someone take the weight of her emotional baggage for a while. When she woke up tomorrow she intended to throw it all away. She was sick of being angry. She was sick of being sad. Neither served her well. She didn't have to hang onto ideas of family when part of that family meant harm to other members. Nothing about that was healthy.

"Do you mind moving to the room I sleep in when I'm home?" Fallon asked. "The guest room doesn't have the same warmth." Fallon found a genuine smile. "My room has a TV. Mom DVR'd every episode of *Blue Bloods* for me."

Max grinned. "Great. Nothing puts me to sleep like family drama masquerading as a police procedural."

"Okay, how about we watch *Midsomer Murder* on Netflix. It's one…" Fallon caught herself. "It *was* one of Mom's favorites. She liked both *Paddington* movies too."

Max came up to her, enveloped her in a hug, and said, "*Blue Bloods* it is."

...

The morning of Summer O'Hara's memorial service was bright and warm. The perfect summer morning with chickadees chirping and water fowl singing their greeting to the day. Most of the tourists were already greeting the day on their bikes, sitting outside drinking coffee and eating cherry crepes at cafés, or teeing off on a dewy, green course.

The street in front of Summer's church was teeming with people. Max and Fallon walked there from Summer's house after the coffee, toast, and eggs Max had whipped up for them. To Fallon's surprise, she'd been famished. Apparently, woman could not survive on ice cream alone.

Finn came up to Fallon first. Kissed her cheek. "Ready for this?" he asked, smiling.

"Not even a little bit." Fallon looked around. "Where's Gus?"

"He's at the winery. He's getting everything ready for the reception after this."

"Isn't he planning on showing up? How's it going to look if he misses his mother's service?"

Finn looked down at her, he wasn't much taller than she was, just tall enough to make her feel small. "Gus is leaving the winery and gallery. He got an offer to head the management team at one of the large estate wineries near Niagara-on-the-Lake. He's leaving at the end of week. He's just getting things in order before he goes."

"He's moving to Canada?" Fallon asked, shaken.

Finn nodded. "It's been brewing for a long time. He needs the time away." Finn looked out over the small crowd milling in front of the church. "Frankly, I could use a little distance from Gus."

"You're not sorry to see him go?"

"Running things without him will be challenging for a while, but it's time. Gus has to find his own way. He needs to forgive himself for the way he treated you. For the way he used Mom to hurt you. I don't think he ever really got over dad's death or Geoff's. Seeing you again solidified his decision. It's time for him to grow up. He can't, or won't, do that here."

Fallon linked her arm with Finn's. "You've got a good heart, brother-mine. Definitely the best of us. Shall we go tell everyone how wonderful our quirky, gem-obsessed, wig-wearing, rum-drinking mother once was?"

"That woman you described is the one we'll be saying hello to when this is over. Let's go say goodbye to the woman who spent too much time alone, whose life was on standby, waiting to hear about her grown children's day. I'm happy to say goodbye to that woman if we get to welcome the woman Rolly brought out. I want Mom to be happy. She's way too young to act so old."

And that's what they did. They said goodbye to the woman who defined herself by the men she'd loved and lost, and said hello to the one she'd let play since dying. Fallon shook her head, she fervently hoped that almost dying had jolted her mother back into living life well.

Fallon stopped and looked around at the town she'd been raised in, taking in the community, the landscape, the sights and sounds and scents of home. Not everything she needed was here, but the most important things were.

They were hiding in plain sight.

CHAPTER TWELVE

"Life is a grand adventure, Jack. Always has been, always will be," said the woman in the long blond wig as she walked into Jack Smith's shop. She had expertly picked the lock and now locked it again behind her. She pulled the shade on the front door, making the interior a little dimmer than before. The store was still filled with light from all the west and southern facing windows, none of which had shades to pull. But the woman knew that. She was making a point. Giving Jack fair warning.

"Sign on the door says closed for a funeral," Jack said, looking up over his reading glasses from his accounts.

"Didn't think that applied to me," she said, coming closer to the case Jack was standing behind. "Don't worry, Jack. You'll make it to your funeral."

Jack reached for the Walther he kept under the case. He pulled it out, aiming it straight at her. "Didn't have to be this way," he said.

The woman smiled slowly. "We had a good run, Jack. Better than most ever get. But you and I both know it was always going to be this way."

Jack aimed at her head and pulled the trigger.

It landed making a clicking sound. The gun was empty.

The woman made a *tsk* sound. Her smile deepened. This time it reached her eyes. "When your gun don't shoot, it's time to leave the game, Jack. Your gun hasn't shot for quite some time."

Before Jack could reach for the shotgun he kept in a secret compartment in the wall behind him, he felt the cut. She was fast. Precise. The blade so sharp he barely felt it.

Jack touched the side of his neck. Pulling his fingers away, he saw his own blood staining them. It wasn't much. Just a small tear in the skin.

The woman reached into her beach bag and tossed a handful of tiny periwinkle cut flowers. They were lovely— star-shaped with five petals each. He recognized them immediately. They were freshly cut from the small flower garden in front of his shop.

It wasn't the cut that would kill him. Jack realized it the second the flowers hit the glass top of his case. The blade she cut him with was laced with the same poison he'd given Summer O'Hara before pushing her down her stairs. The woman had introduced it directly into his bloodstream.

He'd be seeing Summer O'Hara sooner than he thought, in less than thirty minutes if he didn't get to a hospital. He reached for his cell phone.

The women held up a boxlike devise. "Don't bother. I've jammed the signal."

"Why?" Jack asked.

The woman didn't even try to misunderstand. "Nick

Card is younger than you. He'll be around a long time. He pays better. Did you know about Fallon Murphy's connection to Nick when you poisoned her mother?"

He'd known. Jack made a judgment call. A fatal one. It never occurred to him that Nick Card would place one woman above what was good for business.

That misjudgment cost him his life.

...

The woman stuffed the wig in her bag. She went in the back and cleared out what stones she thought she could use, leaving enough—per Nick Card's instructions—for that FBI agent to find. Case closed. He wouldn't get all the stones, not even the best ones, but he'd get his man.

Hopefully, that would be enough.

Nick asked her to do one more thing on her way out of town.

She did what he asked and disappeared. St. Moritz was lovely this time of year.

CHAPTER THIRTEEN

Fallon walked into the reception with Finn and Max at her side. Tables were laid out with place settings. Warm and cold dishes were spread throughout the shop. The wine bar was stocked with tea and coffee and open, half-corked bottles of Murphy Brother's wine.

Gus was nowhere in sight.

A woman Fallon had never seen before with short black hair and deep green eyes bumped into Max. He steadied her, smiling. His gaze lingered a bit too long. "Do I know you?" he asked.

The flash of jealousy that surged through Fallon irritated her. It was irrational and unwanted. It wasn't like she and Max were really married or that last night meant anything more than two lonely people sharing the night together, staving off the hurt and aloneness that defined both their lives, up until the moment Max approached her at the shore.

A time that could be measured in hours as much as in days.

She had no business feeling jealous.

That didn't stop Fallon from grabbing Max's hand.

The woman, who would have stood apart from the crowd no matter where the crowd was, raised a brow at her, then turned back to Max, ignoring her completely. "No, I don't think we've met. Perhaps we'll meet again." She stumbled on her high heels, catching herself on Max's arm. As soon as she did, she was gone, leaving Max staring after her.

"She isn't that beautiful," Fallon said, regretting the words the second they were out her mouth.

Max looked at Fallon briefly then back toward the space where the woman disappeared. He was searching the crowd when he said, "Yes, she is."

Fallon jerked her hand away.

Max didn't seem to care. He kept scanning the crowd. "That's not it. The way she moved. It…it's familiar…" Max took off at a run. He made it through the side door and into the parking lot before Fallon could call after him.

He scanned the parking lot, seeing the long blond wig in the middle of it. The woman was nowhere in sight. The phone in his suit jacket pocket began to vibrate. Max fished it out. It wasn't his phone. His thumb slid across the surface. He held it to his ear.

"Summer O'Hara can come home now."

"What are you talking about?"

"Don't be obtuse, Max. You're no good at it. The threat's over. No one will come after her or her family. If I were you, I'd stick close to the daughter. If that flash of jealousy is any indication, she's fallen for you already. Don't go chasing stones when you could be catching hearts."

Max said nothing. He continued to scan the immediate area, trying to ignore regret he heard in the woman's smoky voice.

"I'll find you," Max said, knowing that wasn't going to happen anytime soon.

"No," she said. "You won't. Check your jacket, Max. Let the rest go." The phone went dead.

Max reached into his opposite jacket pocket. He pulled out the pendant with the red diamond he purchased from Jack Smith's store. He felt the coldness of loose stones as well. He pulled them out and looked at them, a blue diamond about a carat in size, two small red diamonds, and a yellow cushion cut about 10 carats that he thought was from the Graff theft.

The Flower of Scotland wasn't among the stones.

He was fairly certain it was halfway around the world by now. Max could keep chasing it.

Or he could close this case, a feat made easier by the stones that literally fell into his pocket. Then he could take the woman's advice and start chasing the only heart he cared about.

Fallon came out the side door walking slowly toward him.

"What's wrong?" she asked, stopping at his side.

Max pulled her too him and kissed her. Deeply. Fully. Like she was the only woman in the world and now was the only moment that mattered.

Fallon kissed him back with every ounce of feeling she had in her. There was something urgent in Max's kiss as if he'd made up his mind about something important.

"Tell me what's wrong, Max."

He smiled. Then he threw his head back and laughed. "Not a thing, darling. Not one thing." He kissed her again. "Everything about you makes me smile."

Epilogue

Jack Smith's jewelry shop reopened after his death to wide speculation and acclaim. People came from all over the world to purchase synthetic stones based on the great collector gems they represented. Summer O'Hara-Scott, the woman responsible and the owner of the shop, could be seen there from Memorial Day through Labor Day most summers, telling anyone who would listen all about gems and jewelry. She earned more than enough from her shop to purchase her own fancy colored diamond which she wore on her right hand—a 2 carat yellow diamond in the shape of a heart. She wore that ring until her granddaughter's twenty-first birthday when she gave it and the shop to her.

Fallon's daughter inherited her grandmother's love of jewels and her mother's love of opals. And her grandfather Rolly's love of sailing—a love he had in common with her biological grandfather, Padraig Murphy. In time, she'd name her first son, Roland Patrick, honoring them both.

One day, long after her children were grown, she would inherit her mother's journal.

In that journal, Fallon Murphy Scott, wrote of her joys

and her sorrows, her triumphs, her travels, and her walks on the wild side—a life made possible by balancing her work with Nick Card while loving and living with Max Scott, a stickler for the law.

That journal began with the line: *On what I thought was the worst day of my life, the day I thought my mother died, I looked around me and chose to see what was in plain sight.*

Life is simple.

It's defined by hope and light and holding on to those who make our hearts smile.

It is possible to fall in love in a day—all it takes is a moment of real connection—and to keep that love alive every day for the rest of your life.

I did.

So can you.

About the author:

A native mid-westerner, Leigh lives in Southeastern Wisconsin and is currently dreaming of owning a cottage in Scotland.

Leigh is currently working on a series of stand alone contemporary novels, The Warrior Chronicles, with a tie to the martial arts. Adventure, romance, and themes such as 'what constitutes a family', and 'living by a personal code' all wrapped up in a tail-kicking package that will make you laugh, cry, and feel good about the world and your place in it.

A graduate of Marquette University Law School, Leigh studied Comparative Mythology, History and Philosophy as an undergraduate. Who knew this would lead to a lifetime of love with mystical romance, both contemporary and historical.

Leigh is a fifth degree black belt in Okinawan Shorin Ryu karate. She has continuously trained over a twenty year period with Master Daniel Schroeder in Hales Corners, Wisconsin. She also holds a fifth degree black belt in Matayoshi Okinawan Kobudo; weapons training. Leigh has taught self-defense for women and practical defense sequences for writers.

Leigh is an avid motorcycle enthusiast. (There's nothing like a TRIUMPH or INDIAN!) Most summers (when she's not out riding) you can most likely find her in Highland Gear walking her Scottish Deerhounds and promoting Macski's Highland Foods at local Scottish Games and Festivals.

You may visit Leigh at:
www.leighmorganauthor.com

For speaking engagements and martial arts
seminars, please email Leigh at:
leighmorgan@bardintraining.com

For the best tasting Scottish foods and custom
Highland Gear this side of the big pond please visit:
www.macskis.com